THE QUEST OF EXCALIBUR

BOOKS BY LEONARD WIBBERLEY

Adult Fiction

The Quest of Excalibur
Beware of the Mouse
Take Me to Your President
McGillicuddy McGotham
The Mouse That Roared
Mrs. Searwood's Secret Weapon

Adult Nonfiction

No Garlic in the Soup
The Coming of the Green
The Trouble with the Irish

Juvenile Nonfiction

Wes Powell—Conqueror of the
    Grand Canyon
John Barry—Father of the Navy
The Story of Winston Churchill
The Epics of Everest
The Coronation Book

Juvenile Fiction

Kevin O'Connor and the Light Brigade
The Wound of Peter Wayne
Deadman's Cave
The Secret of the Hawk
The King's Beard
John Treegate's Musket

Leonard Wibberley

THE QUEST
OF
EXCALIBUR

G. P. Putnam's Sons   New York

DEDICATED

*to Ted Erlandson, Chairman of the English Depart-
ment at Loyola University, Los Angeles, who some
years ago suggested a book on the return of Arthur. I
am indebted to him for the basic idea and to my friend
Robert Nathan for his advice on the manuscript.*

THE AUTHOR

Foreword

And for to passe the tyme thys book shal be plesaunte to rede in, but for to gyve fayth and byleve that al is trewe that is conteyned herein, ye be at your lyberte. But al is wryton for our doctryne, and for to beware that we falle not to vyce ne synne, but t'exersyse and folowe vertu, by whyche we may come and atteyne to good fame and renomme in thys lyf, and after thys shorte and transytorye lyf to cme unto everlastyng blysse in heven the whyche He graunte us that reygneth in heven, the Blessyd Trynyte.

Amen

(From Caxton's Preface to works of Sir Thomas Malory)

BOOK I

The Return of the King

Chapter One

CIBBER BROWN was cleaning the mud off his spade with a stick of hazelwood in a methodical manner and contemplating the prospect of fried rabbit for dinner. A young fried rabbit with thick brown gravy and some mushrooms and two big slices of bread spread heavy with margarine would go uncommonly well for dinner if taken with a pint of Somerset cider to wash it down, he thought.

When he, Cibber Brown, was a boy hardly a summer week went by but there was rabbit pie or rabbit stew or fried rabbit on every countryman's table. But nowadays people thought of rabbits as they thought of rats.

Once, before the Ministry of Agriculture had undertaken to exterminate them, there had been rabbits aplenty in England, and you could take a gun into a field any evening and shoot yourself a couple of them and sell the pelts for sixpence the piece. Or you could tuck a brace of white ferrets in your pocket and whistle to your dog and go along any hedgerow and get rabbits merely by putting the ferrets down the holes and letting the dog catch them when the panicked rabbits burst from the earth like souls on Resurrection Day.

Meanwhile you smoked your pipe—he himself preferred an aromatic flake tobacco—and looked around at the tangle of roots and holes at the bottom of the hedge and the little plants and flowers there: hensbane and Queen Anne's lace and lass-a-milking and any number of flowers that people these days didn't know the names of.

You looked at the hedge and then at the fields around with the long shadows on them and every tuft of grass covered with a halo and every tree heavy with summer growth. And as you looked you listened to the jolly rowdy chirpings of hedge sparrows and the bad-tempered chatter of finches and now and again the flute notes of a blackbird. And doing all this you felt warmed and strengthened. It was a good way to feel, that; watching the glorious and majestic advance of an English summer's evening and smoking your pipe and at any moment expecting to nab a couple of rabbits for dinner.

When the spade was cleaned, Cibber threw away the hazel stick, looked slowly along the line of ditch which he had cleared of mud and weeds and sedges that day and whistled to Toby, his dog. Toby padded over to him and Cibber picked up his workcoat, which was hung on a blackthorn bush, and his basket, which contained his thermos flask, and set off for his house on the other side of Glastonbury.

His way led through the ruins of Glastonbury Abbey, and

the gates surrounding the ruins had not yet been locked. Cibber looked forward to his walk through the ruins every evening. It gave him a pleasant feeling, a sense, though he could not quite define it, of belonging to a huge stream of life which came strongly out of the remote past and plunged strongly on into the unseeable future.

There was little enough left of the Abbey, which had been one of the most glorious in England. There were just a few gray stones which roughly outlined where the walls had stood. The Prior's kitchen was in fair shape, but the rest of the Abbey was just a residual trace. And yet there was a feeling of both holiness and antiquity; a feeling of faith and serenity and abiding strength which deeply comforted Cibber Brown whenever he passed through.

He went slowly, thinking vaguely of rabbits and monks and pilgrims and the many legends which attached to Glastonbury Abbey. Joseph of Arimathaea, who had given his own sepulcher for the burial of Christ, was held to have been its founder. He had come from the Holy Land to England and put his staff in the ground hereabouts and it had flowered in midwinter into a blackthorn bush. The Abbey had been built on the site of the miracle.

All around, in those days, had been a big lake and the Abbey, on a hill, had then been on an island. Far away to the east on another island had been Camelot, the castle of King Arthur. Arthur was rowed in a barge across the lake from Camelot to Glastonbury many a time to visit the monks and worship in the Abbey. When Arthur died, one of his knights had taken his sword, Excalibur, and thrown it into the lake.

Maybe it was still lying around somewhere. Cibber Brown sometimes thought that it was just possible that *he* might find the sword Excalibur himself. He might be digging away somewhere—maybe cutting a new ditch at the orders of the Rural District Council—through a part that had never been dug before, and his spade might strike something metallic. And when he lifted the spade up, out would come this sword, glittering like the moon on the water, and the glow of it lighting the air around it like a halo.

A little shiver of delight passed through him at the thought of so magical a thing happening. He didn't know what he would do with the sword if he ever found it. His daydreaming never carried him that far. All he knew was what he would not do with it. And one of the things he would not do with it was turn it over to Mr. Joseph Melton, chairman of the Glastonbury Rural District Council and a Nosy Parker of astonishing talent.

It seemed that Mr. Melton knew just about everything that went on among the workers of the District Council, and took an especial delight in inquiring into the whereabouts and activities of the council's only ditcher—Cibber Brown.

As bad luck would have it, he met Mr. Melton now, halfway across the two or three acres of greensward around which the pathetic ruins of Glastonbury Abbey were scattered. As usual Mr. Melton, a small lean man with a thin mouth and a faint ginger mustache, had a mackintosh over his arm, an umbrella in his hand, and a bowler hat on his head. These were almost the badges of his office, like the mace and crown and mantle of sovereigns. The mackintosh signified that Mr. Melton, in the course of his duties, was out in all weathers. The bowler hat signified that he was of the executive class which rules the cloth-capped class to which Cibber Brown belonged. And the umbrella proved that he did not work with his hands, for no English workman from time immemorial has ever been known to carry an umbrella.

"Evening, Cibber," said Mr. Melton, with the smile common to executioners sharpening their axes. "Knocked off a little early today, didn't you?"

"Evening," said Cibber. "Knocked off when I'd done a day's work. Two hundred yards of ditching is enough for any man in one day."

"You're paid by the hour and should work by the hour," said Mr. Melton. "By the way, I see that you are carrying your spade. You know that the by-laws insist that all tools be turned in to the council toolshed and must not be carried home by workmen."

Cibber Brown said nothing to this. He had brought the spade with him because he was going rabbiting. He would need the spade to stop some of the holes in the rabbit warren to give his dog less work to do. But such an explanation wouldn't go down with Mr. Melton, he knew.

"I think you'd better take the spade back to the toolshed," said Mr. Melton. "It is public property, you know, and not to be used for private purposes. I'd watch my step if I were you. Certain members of the District Council are coming to the conclusion that it would be less expensive to buy a ditching machine than to employ a ditcher. Leaving your job early and taking public property home with you is likely to have a bearing on their thinking. Evening."

He gave a sharp nod and strode off.

Cibber Brown watched Mr. Melton's back and from this turned to contemplate the spade. Should he return it to the toolshed? Melton was sure to find out if he didn't. Or should he keep it and go rabbiting anyway?

The matter was complicated by the fact that Melton was Cibber Brown's brother-in-law. This brought into their relationship an unspoken ill-feeling. Melton's upper-middle-class pride made him ashamed of the fact that his brother-in-law was a ditch digger and quite content to remain one. He did not like to entertain ditch diggers at his table and discouraged Cibber from visiting his sister Mary, Melton's wife. Cibber, on the other hand, was fond of his sister and resented being cut off from her as well as the humiliations she received at her husband's hands.

All this then was involved in the matter of Cibber Brown's employment and in the problem of whether he should return the Rural District Council's spade to the Rural District Council's toolshed. He stood among the Abbey ruins and thought about it. And, because of the mood conjured up by the ruins, he thought also about King Arthur and the West Country belief that one day he would return. Cibber wished heartily that he would.

From the northern foot of the hill upon which the ruins stood, a lark leaped suddenly out of the daisies and flung itself into the sky, chattering on fluttering wings. Cibber watched it carefully. It was fluttering in an agitated, protesting kind of way and had risen to no great height. When the bird returned to the ground it did not drop in one dramatic swoop but came down fluttering as it had gone up.

"T'will rain in a couple of hours," said Cibber to himself. "Rain or turn all cloudy and misty." He looked over to the east where four meadows rose in quiet succession to a copse of beech, oak, hemlock, elm and hazelwood. He caught a glimpse of a white flash at the edge of the copse—nothing more than the smallest ball of white, as it were, and it was gone.

Rabbits.

There was a colony of them over there that had somehow escaped the extermination attempt of the Ministry of Agriculture. The copse was on the land of Sir Timothy Bors. Indeed, it was all the land that remained to Sir Timothy, and so he, Cibber, could not go rabbiting on it without poaching.

But what was rabbiting without poaching anyway? In any case there wasn't a great deal of risk. Sir Timothy, impoverished by taxes, was reduced to a Rolls Royce, vintage '21, which he could not afford to drive, this small copse and a manor house of which he occupied only two rooms. Sir Timothy certainly couldn't afford a gamekeeper for the tiny copse which was all that remained of some thousand acres which had belonged to the Bors family for a thousand years.

"I'll keep the spade and go poaching," said Cibber Brown. "And if I catch a couple of rabbits, I'll give one to Sir Timothy. No doubt he'd be grateful for it, being a nobleman and out of work."

Chapter Two

CIBBER BROWN kept the two ferrets he would need for his rabbiting in a cage in the back garden of his small cottage, a place of only three rooms—a bedroom, kitchen and bathroom. The ferrets, pink-eyed, snakelike and yellow-haired, were curled up in the straw of their cage. They had upset their bowl of water as usual, so that the straw was damp, and they shivered deliciously when Cibber picked them up and popped them in the pocket of his jacket. Ferrets liked the dark, Cibber knew well, for pink eyes are not made for daylight hunting. The two ferrets crouched in the bottom of his pocket, still trembling, though not perhaps so much with cold as with anticipation. The pockets of their master's jacket they associated with hunting; with streaking down the winding burrows of rabbits and rats, now pausing to sniff, now listening, now stopping with whiskers atremble, feeling as it were the very nerves of air around, and then plunging onward to where the smell or sound of rabbit or rats beckoned them.

Having obtained his ferrets, Cibber filled a worn leather tobacco pouch with his favorite aromatic flake tobacco, put four matches in the top pocket of his jacket and picked up a stick of ash with a polished knot at one end, which was the very weapon for rabbiting. He didn't give a thought to the single-barrel shotgun which stood in the corner of the living room. It was no weapon to take poaching and, in any case, cartridges were expensive.

It occurred to him as he was about to leave that his rabbiting might take longer than he anticipated. He didn't like to be hurried about anything, nor set a time for the ending of any particular activity. Therefore it would be wise to bring along something to eat. So he cut a chunk off a loaf of bread and added to this a large piece of yellow cheese. These he wrapped in a bandana handkerchief and put them under his cloth cap.

All being now ready, he left the cottage heading for Sir Timothy's copse. He passed northward of the Abbey ruins, across a couple of pastures and then downward into the rank and matted grasses of the area which had once been the bottom of a lake. The going here was not easy, though Cibber was used to such terrain. Continued ditching round about had produced a kind of thick mud surface out of which the sedge grasses and rushes grew. But he had to be careful where he put his feet, for there were many bogholes around, and carelessness could result in getting mud up to his knees, and that in a second. Cibber moved slowly, the Rural District Council's spade over his shoulder, his stick in one hand and his dog, Toby, follow-

ing him, making jumps from hummock to hummock, occasionally missing his footing and falling foolishly into some muddy
area.

At this time of the year the bog was knee-high with marsh
marigold which left its yellow dust on his boots and trousers
as Cibber walked along. Here and there were a few wild hya-
cinth and there were occasional stretches of wild iris—yellow
when they bloomed, not blue like the ones people raised in
their gardens.

A few frogs croaked, impatient for the evening, and coming
to a shallow pool, Cibber surprised a mallard and her chicks
grubbing for food in the muddy bottom. The chicks, so anxious
to get away that they forgot for a moment how to fly, splashed
and fluttered in the water. The dull-plumed mother gave a
squawk and tried to shepherd them to the sedges opposite.
And suddenly out of the sky came the drake, blue and black
and white-banded, and fierce. He circled like a bullet around
Cibber, offering himself as a target for the safety of his family
and when they had reached the protection of the rushes, landed
in a little pool beyond, still drawing attention to himself by
quacking loudly.

Cibber, ignoring the ducks, walked quietly along the edge of
this pool whose surface was covered with pale green platelets
of water weeds and the tongue-thick, deep green leaves of
water lilies.

The lilies were in full bloom, only the tips of their slightly
pink petals breaking the surface of the water. The rest of the
bloom, serene, remote, beautiful, lay in the crystal depths.
A fierce blue dragonfly with a scarlet head and monstrous

transparent wings zoomed over one of the lily pads and was gone. Four lazy bubbles of marsh gas floated up through the water near the bank on which Cibber was standing. They came up as perfect silver spheres and in their bursting sent tiny ever-widening rings over the surface of the water. On summer nights sometimes this gas, by some means which Cibber did not know, caught fire, and then a pale blue flame which was called a will-o'-the-wisp, floated gently over the marshlands, appearing and disappearing while the night around watched in silence.

These little happenings in the pool, quietly watched, greatly soothed Cibber Brown, and he might have remained by the pool for much longer but that one of the ferrets thrust a quivering pink nose out of his pocket to remind him that he had set out to do some rabbiting and the evening was getting on.

He looked over to the northwest where the big generous neck of the Severn River divulged into the Bristol Channel and noted that the sun, though still well above the horizon, was coppery and that a breath of mist was gathering in the lowlands. The lark had been right. The weather was about to turn cold and cloudy and there'd be a heavy ground mist in an hour or so.

He clucked to Toby and went on toward the copse, walking no faster but now not lingering to watch anything he passed.

It was a little after eight when he got to the woods, to judge by the sun. There was still a couple of hours before the midsummer sunset, but a cloudbank had formed in the west and so there would be a long and gloomy twilight.

That twilight made itself felt immediately Cibber broke

through the growth of brambles and hazel bushes that formed the outer wall of the copse. Inside the light was dulled and the very fact that it was subdued seemed to increase the wood smells around—smells of leaves and fungi and sap and crushed grass and mold.

Cibber had no difficulty in finding the rabbit warren. It was in a bank about two feet high, grown over with elderberry bushes. It was an old warren and many of the holes had collapsed through disuse. But he inspected the various entrances closely and found four well cleaned but with little particles of black dirt at their mouths, and beyond that, a few rabbit droppings. These four then were in use and Toby sniffed at them and started digging furiously, so fresh was the scent around.

Cibber took one of the ferrets out of his pocket. He showed it to the dog, who sniffed cautiously and backed off distrustingly.

" 'Ware ferret," said Cibber. "You and him's partners. Down you go." He put the ferret to the rabbit hole and it had gone in an instant.

Cibber produced the other ferret and went through the same performance, introducing it to the dog and then letting it down the hole. Toby would know now to leave the ferrets alone and concentrate on any rabbits that were started.

Cibber now considered whether he ought to stop up some of the holes. This would give Toby fewer places to watch and would also make it easier to recover the ferrets who had a perverse habit of refusing to emerge from a warren anywhere near the place they had entered. He took his spade and shouldered his way through the elderberries, stooping low and stopping up a hole or two. He was still engaged in this work when Toby barked and a voice called out from the other side of the bank. "I say. Are you really poaching? Can't have that, you know. This is my property. Not much of it, but, as I say, it's mine."

Cibber backed out of the bushes and confronted Sir Timothy Bors, two hundred and seventeenth Count of Weddon and Earst, to give him but a portion of his title. Sir Timothy was wearing a pair of elderly corduroy trousers of the type common to English agricultural laborers, a venerable Harris tweed jacket and a porkpie hat. He was a rotund man, red in the jowls and with a face as plain and forthright as a side of mutton. He had about him that air of slightly untidy quality which is the birth gift of the English nobility.

"What makes you think I'm poaching?" asked Cibber, trusting that the two ferrets, unreliable creatures at the best of times, would not choose this moment to appear from the warren and undo him.

"Well, you are, aren't you?" countered Sir Timothy with a note almost of pleading in his voice. "I mean you wouldn't be here stopping up rabbit holes on my property just for exercise, would you? After rabbits, I suppose?" he added eagerly.

"Well," confessed Cibber, "I had a fancy for a dish of fried rabbit for dinner."

"My dear fellow," said Sir Timothy, "I regard you as a personal benefactor. Pray continue. Indeed, let me be of assistance."

"Rabbits multiplying too fast?" asked Cibber, surprised at this turn for he had expected to be escorted back to the manor house and handed over to the police.

"Not at all," said Sir Timothy. "It would take a little while to explain. Sit down a minute, and I'll see what I can do to clear it all up and show what a compliment you have paid me in coming here."

The two seated themselves on the bank and Sir Timothy, having cleared his throat and hemmed and hawed a couple of times, launched into his explanation.

"I trust you won't think me a snob," he said, "if I start by pointing out that my family has held land around this area—thousands of acres of land at one time—for fourteen hundred years or more. I take it that you are a fair-minded kind of fellow and will not hold it against me that it has been my lot to be born of a long line of the landed nobility of England."

"Tain't any fault of yours that I can see," said Cibber.

"Ah," said Sir Timothy, "that's very kind of you indeed, old fellow. For you see I *am* a nobleman, and it's a hard thing indeed to be a nobleman, that is to say, born a nobleman and with nothing you can do to alter it, even suppose you wanted to, at a time when the nobility is regarded as the dross of the nation.

"We were not always thought of in this most unreasonable manner. Not so long ago the nobility were looked to as the natural leaders of the whole of England, and instructors of the nation in matters both of honor and manners. Grouse to be shot only in September; human beings only after an official declaration of war. I'm not boring you with all this am I, old man?"

"No," said Cibber, "but I don't see what this has got to do with poaching rabbits."

"Well, maybe I have gone rather far afield," said Sir Timothy. "But I've had this on my mind for a long time and no one to talk to about it. By poaching rabbits in my copse you paid me the compliment of acknowledging that I am still one of the landed nobility of England. Nobody, my dear man, has thought it worth while to poach a rabbit around here for twenty years. You have brought back to me a momentary glimpse of what were, from my point of view, older and better days, when my father employed a dozen gamekeepers as a precaution against poachers, and when the nobility of England, rather than having to apologize for their presence, had inherited rights which they were prepared to defend openly, publicly and with vigor in any court in England—or the world, for that matter.

"And that brings me to the very crux of the matter. Your decision to poach here tonight has sharply brought to my attention the fact that the nobility of England has shamefully failed in its duty toward the commons."

"You mean that you should make your lands, what's left of them, public property?" asked Cibber.

"Perish the thought," said Sir Timothy. "You completely miss my point. We have failed the commons in not insisting upon our status as nobles. We have neglected our sacred trust to be above the rest of the people so as to provide them with leadership in every field. We have abdicated our rights and our privileges to the great hurt of the untitled people of England. In short, we have in an excess of brotherly love become common, which is all right for commoners but positively indecent in noblemen. And all this must be stopped. It has gone too far already."

"I won't go so far as to say that you're right," said Cibber. "And then again I won't go so far as to say that you're wrong."

"Spoken like an Englishman," said Sir Timothy heartily.

"What I mean is that you can't bring back all them barons that ruled England in olden times," continued Cibber. "People won't hold for it these days."

"My dear fellow," said Sir Timothy, "nothing could be further from my mind. What I look to do is to restore some chivalry to England, some nobility of mind, some loftiness of viewpoint, some politeness and honor and charity. These are the tasks of the nobility, and in these tasks, I say to my shame, I and my fellows have in the past failed."

"Chivalry," said Cibber gloomily, thinking of Mr. Melton and the spade. "You've got a point there."

"Of course I have," said Sir Timothy. "The trouble is that we need a leader. Not that I'm not capable of leading *you*. That goes without question. I have no qualms on that score. But who's to lead me? That's the rub. Frankly, old man, what with one thing and another, I'm rather out of touch with what constitutes the public duties of a nobleman, though I set an excellent example for my butler when I had one. But in public matters I haven't had much practice or training as a result of my kind of people being unwanted for so long—except of course for ceremonial occasions."

"Ah," said Cibber, thinking of Glastonbury Abbey and all associated with it, "if only Arthur would come back like the old prophecy said he would. 'E's the one could lead us all."

"Arthur?" echoed Sir Timothy. "You mean King Arthur? Ah yes, there was a king, indeed. You know there hasn't been a quest in England—ignoring for the moment the search for that fellow who won the football pool and was found living under an assumed name with his secretary at Blackpool—since Arthur went away. He would be the very man for the job. We sorely need him now."

A mist, white as samite, had flowed over the marshlands while they talked and now swirled around the higher land of the copse as tidal waters creep up the shores of an island.

The two watched the mist in silence and then saw a long

dark shape, like a barge, slowly appear, which seemed to rock gently as if upon the slightly disturbed surface of a lake. There were three figures in the barge, cloaked and indistinct and yet conveying an impression that they were women, and beautiful women. And standing beside the barge, hip-deep in the mist, was the figure of a man, tall and slender and clad also in a cloak.

Chapter Three

CIBBER BROWN and Sir Timothy recognized King Arthur immediately he entered the copse, stepping from the lake of mist over which he had floated in the barge. Sir Timothy went down on one knee and felt quite natural doing this, for the reaction had been bred in him for fourteen centuries. It was strongly in his genes and he was comforted to find a king to whom he could make obeisance.

Cibber on the other hand did nothing but remove his cloth cap which he held against his chest. He did not go on one knee for while the tradition of the English nobility calls for genuflection, the tradition of the English peasant is that he will bow to nobody, and feels that he betrays his whole class if he does so.

So Cibber stood with his cap to his chest, the only mark of respect permitted him without a betrayal of his kind, and stared at the King.

He saw a man in the full force of his early thirties; a man so perfectly proportioned that it was only by measuring him against one of the lower branches of a nearby beech that Cibber realized that the King was well over six feet tall.

The King's hair hung down to his shoulders and was raven black, as was the hair of the early Celts before their blood was mingled with that of the fair-haired Saxons and Jutes and Angles. His beard was black too, a full black mane that came down to his chest and gave him an authority and majesty as strong as that of a lion. He wore a cape which was fastened by a cord of golden cloth around his shoulders and under this, a tunic of doeskin. The cloak was dark, but little globules of mist clung to it, scintillating little spheres which caught the light of the stars and turned it into a white fire. Arthur then was outlined in a cold, pure light. Across the King's shoulders hung a baldric and from it, the top just visible under the cloak, was hung a big jeweled scabbard.

The scabbard was empty and Cibber knew that this was the scabbard which had once held the King's wondrous sword Excalibur.

"Tell me what knight thou art and where lies thy castle," said King Arthur to Sir Timothy.

"Sire," said Sir Timothy rising and dusting off his corduroys, "I am Sir Timothy Bors, Count of Weddon and Earst, Warden of the Western Marches, High Steward of the Stanneries, Royal Capon Butler and Server of Ewry, and Hereditary Headholder to the Monarch of England when upon the High Seas."

"These other offices I know, but not this last," said King

Arthur. "What manner of office is this of Headholder of the Monarch of England when upon the High Seas?"

"It happened, by your leave, Sire," replied Sir Timothy, "that when King John, who came after you, was on his way to France to visit his estates, he was taken seasick and suffered grievously. Whereupon one of my ancestors did the king the service of holding his head over the side of the vessel when the need arose, and that service has been hereditary in my family now for eight hundred years."

The reply seemed to satisfy Arthur for he turned now to Cibber and said, "Who's churl are you, fellow?"

"The Rural District Council's," said Cibber.

"This is some kind of a monastery?" Arthur asked.

The thought had never occurred to Cibber before. But now that it was presented to him he recognized that this was exactly what the Rural District Council was—a closed society of clerkly fellows controlling a large acreage, opening drains, laying down roads, uprooting property, all with such righteousness that one would think the Lord Himself was their chairman.

"It is a kind of a monastery indeed," replied Cibber.

"Do you have a name, fellow?" asked the King.

"I do," was the reply. "Cibber Brown."

"Was it you who called to me to come back from Avalon?"

"Yes," said Cibber. "Me and Sir Timothy here."

"Then I have come, churl, to your succor for it is the part of a king to come to the aid of those oppressed. But let us go up to the Castle of Sir Timothy and there you may lay your petition before me."

"If you don't mind, I'd like to get my ferrets first," said Cibber.

"They are there," said the King and pointed. And there were the two ferrets with Toby between them. Toby had a fat rabbit in his mouth.

"Good," said Cibber, "we can have rabbit for dinner after all."

He had stopped to pick up the rabbit and, getting no comment on the proposed menu, turned. Arthur and Sir Timothy had gone and Cibber was there in the mist alone, wondering whether he had been dreaming.

He stood quite still for a while and looked around at the deep velvet shadows of the trees, given shape only by the silver starshine on their topmost bowers, and at the white mist which still swirled around like the ghosts of England's history, and at the clump of elderberries, black now as witches' brooms.

"Maybe I ought to call them," he said to Toby. He cupped his hands to his mouth and called, "Arthur! Arthur! Where are you?"

Out of the mist there came a muffled thumping as of someone running, and two figures loomed up and pounced on him. One was Mr. Melton and the other was a police constable.

"I'm afraid I'm going to have to take you in," said the constable, not unkindly. "Poaching's against the law."

"And poaching with the Rural District Council's equipment is a felony," said Mr. Melton triumphantly.

"If I could see Sir Timothy Bors it would be all right," said Cibber. "He would explain everything."

The constable looked queerly at Melton and then at Cibber. "Sir Timothy Bors?" he said.

"Yes. Him that owns the manor house at the other end of the copse."

The constable took off his helmet and scratched his head and then put the helmet back on. Having in this manner indicated his surprise, he said, "Sir Timothy Bors died two hours ago in London. Nasty business. Be all over the papers tomorrow."

"Died?" exclaimed Cibber.

"What happened?" asked Mr. Melton.

"Well," said the constable, "speaking unofficially" (and he took off his helmet to indicate that this was indeed the case), "it seems that Sir Timothy was taken with returning to the days of what you might call chivalry. He went to his flat in London and put on a suit of armor that belonged to one of his ancestors and went charging out into the streets. It was four o'clock in the morning and he got knocked down by a milk van and died in the hospital late this afternoon."

"Did he say anything before he died to explain this er ... ahem ... aberration?" asked Melton.

"Not what you might call 'explain' it," said the constable. "He said, 'Arthur! Arthur! Cannot I break one lance for England?'"

"Hardly makes sense," sniffed Mr. Melton.

"Makes sense to me, though," said Cibber. "He had his duties as a nobleman."

To his surprise, the constable agreed.

Chapter Four

JUSTICE of the Peace Henry Beauchamp, stipendiary magistrate of the lower court at Glastonbury, was a man with the wholesome conviction that the whole foundation of British justice rested upon the most thorough investigation of even the pettiest cases.

Like the bulk of British magistrates of the older school, he had no formal legal training. Indeed his business was that of corn merchant, and in this business he had spent thirty-five years of his life and had prospered.

He had, however, been twenty years on the magistrate's bench and could find his way around the laws and by-laws of the county with the same ease that he found his way around the sacks of meal, corn, oats and oilcake which were stacked in his warehouses.

But he was no stickler for law, holding the proper view that, while the law may be a limb of justice, it does not in itself constitute the whole body.

"Judgment," he would say, "is a human function and may not be circumscribed by statute. If matters were otherwise, we might readily file the facts of any case into a machine containing every statute on the law books of this realm, press a button, receive from it an impartial, mechanical and inhuman verdict."

When Cibber Brown then was arraigned before the magistrate on the dual counts of poaching and misappropriation of public property in the form of the spade of the Glastonbury Rural District Council, Beauchamp was as determined to have as full an investigation of the charges as if they had been as serious as murder or high treason.

The charge was read to the court by the magistrate's clerk, and Mr. Beauchamp asked Cibber whether he had heard it and whether he understood it.

"Yes, Mr. Beauchamp," said Cibber.

"There is no individual by the name of Beauchamp in this court," said the magistrate. "If you wish to address the bench, you should say 'Your Honor.' "

"Yes, Your Honor," said Cibber.

"Are you represented by legal counsel?" asked the magistrate.

"No," said Cibber and he explained that he didn't wish a lawyer. He pleaded guilty to the charge of misappropriation of the spade but not guilty to the charge of poaching.

"Let us address ourselves then," said the magistrate, "to the poaching charge."

The constable and Mr. Melton had soon given their evidence, Mr. Melton stressing that he had met Cibber, told him to take the spade back to the toolshed, warned him that he had no right to use it after working hours, and had subsequently been informed that Cibber had been seen walking with the spade in the direction of Sir Timothy's copse. He had thereupon assumed that Cibber was engaged in an illegal pursuit and had gone to the police station and only obtained the services of a constable after some delay. He and Constable Andrew Rawlins, assigned to the case, had caught the defendant red-handed and the arrest had been made.

He took leave to ask the court to take a severe view of the matter. Although it might be argued that only a spade was involved, the principle was one of the protection of public property and a man who misappropriated a spade one day, might misappropriate a truck the next.

Melton showed some signs of expanding on this theme but was cut off by the magistrate with the remark that the defendant, being tried for a spade, was not to be tried at the same time for any tendencies to walk off with the crown jewels of England. That could be attended to if and when the matter arose.

Cibber then took the stand.

"On the charge of poaching," said the magistrate, "you have pleaded not guilty. What do you have to say to substantiate your plea?"

Cibber looked around the little courtroom hoping to find a friendly or at least a receptive face. But the only person there who seemed at all well disposed to him was his sister, Mary, sitting in the back of the court and wringing her handkerchief, and undoubtedly in greater need of comfort than himself.

"What I've got to say is going to sound funny," said Cibber.

"The court will be the judge of that," said Mr. Beauchamp. "Pray proceed."

"Well," said Cibber, "poaching means taking game on private premises without the permission of the owner, don't it?"

"It does indeed."

"Well, I ain't guilty because I had the permission of the owner. He was right there with me."

"Sir Timothy Bors?" said the magistrate, starting forward in his chair.

"That's right," said Cibber. "He came along while me ferrets was down the warren and I was stopping up a few holes. And he halfway begged me to keep on poaching and said he'd be glad to help, and that I was doing him a favor because he was a nobleman and nobody had poached on his land for twenty years."

Everybody in the courtroom knew Sir Timothy Bors and knew that he had died some hours before Cibber was arrested for poaching. A buzz of talk filled the place and Cibber's sister, Mary, was so affected that she got to her feet and called out, "Oh, Cibber," making the "Oh" into a wail of despair as if he had been guilty of a final outrage against truth after a lifetime spent in prevarication.

"It's true, Mary," Cibber said, over the hubbub, seeking to comfort her.

"Silence," the magistrate burst out, forgetting his gavel in the excitment of the moment and slapping his big meaty palm upon the bench. "Silence in court. Silence, I say. I'll impose a fine of five shillings for contempt on the next person who utters a word."

Few were prepared to risk the loss of five shillings for the privilege of further discussing even so exciting a development and silence was soon restored.

"Now, sir," said the magistrate turning to Cibber, "you realize that you are giving testimony under oath?"

"Yes, Your Honor."

"And you have told the court that you received permission from Sir Timothy Bors to take rabbits on his estate—is that not so?"

"Yes, Your Honor."

"Are you aware, sir, that Sir Timothy Bors was dead at the time you say that he gave you this er ... miraculous permission? Clerk, delete that word 'miraculous.' It smacks of prejudice on the bench. My apologies to the defendant. I will rephrase my question. Are you aware that Sir Timothy Bors was dead at the time that you say he er ... at the time you say that you saw him?"

"I wasn't aware then, sir," said Cibber. " 'E didn't look dead to me. 'Ealthy I'd call 'im. In 'is prime. But I was told by Andie there, I mean Constable Rawlins, that 'e was dead. That was at the time of my arrest, sir."

"And what do you say to that?"

"Well, Your Honor, it appears that being dead don't make much difference to a man, like parson says in church."

A guffaw from the spectators was quickly silenced by the magistrate.

"Are you trying to tell the court that Sir Timothy Bors returned from the grave for the express purpose of giving you permission to poach rabbits on his estate?" the magistrate asked. He was becoming annoyed because he felt that the situation was getting out of hand and the defendant seemed intent upon making a farce out of a serious legal inquiry.

"No, sir," said Cibber. "I don't say that that was his reason for coming back from the grave. But I do say that he were there and gave me permission as I told you."

A new idea occurred to Mr. Beauchamp. "Is it possible that you mistook someone else for Sir Timothy?" he asked. "Are you well acquainted with Sir Timothy's appearance and the sound of his voice?"

"I've seen him a number of times," said Cibber, "but this was the first time I ever spoke to him."

For a while defendant and magistrate looked at each other, the one abashed but dogged and the other openly dubious.

Then Mr. Beauchamp glanced around the court and said, "I'm going to dismiss the charge of poaching, for the defendant has created some measure of doubt as to whether someone whom he took for Sir Timothy Bors did or did not give him permission to take rabbits on Sir Timothy's land. The defendant is entitled to the benefit of this doubt and therefore is declared innocent of this charge. There are no witnesses to show that he did *not* talk to somebody, though the court cannot tolerate for a moment any nonsense about that person being Sir Timothy Bors.

"On the second charge that the defendant misappropriated public property in the form of a spade which he took with him, there is no doubt in my mind that he did so and indeed the defendant himself admits this. I must therefore, under the law, fine the defendant one shilling which is the minimum fine allowable under the regulations.

"The court is dismissed."

There was an immediate milling and jostling of the spectators around the clerk of the court, all of them anxious to pay Cibber Brown's fine and shake Cibber's hand, for he was popular in Glastonbury and had provided an amusing hour or so in the courtroom.

They winked at Cibber for having, as they thought, put one over on the magistrate, or maybe because they thought he had been caught in a bad lie and been dealt with leniently. Then, smiling, they drifted off to discuss the matter at the local over a pint of cider or maybe a glass of ale.

Chapter Five

IMMEDIATELY after his trial Cibber went down to the District Council office, interviewed the works foreman and quit his job. He didn't give any reason why he wished to leave and he was not pressed for one. It was assumed that he was exasperated at being hauled into court over so small an offense as borrowing the Rural District Council's spade.

When he had collected his pay, he stopped around at Melton's house to see his sister, Mary.

"I'll be going away for a while," he said. "Here's a couple of quid for you. Look after yourself until I get back. See that my ferrets are fed and take care of the dog for me. Ferrets need raw meat but don't overfeed them or they'll get lazy."

"Oh Cibber," said his sister, "I'm always so worried about you. What are you going to do?"

"Don't rightly know," replied Cibber. "I'm going to find out."

"You won't be going to London, will you?" his sister asked and with some excitement. It would give her great pleasure if she could just mention casually to her husband that Cibber had gone to London, for Somerset people who had been to London gained some prestige from this. Melton had never been there.

"Maybe," said Cibber. "But more likely I'll be going to Camelot."

"Camelot?" said Mary, surprised. Cibber nodded, gave her a pat on her thin, nervous hands and went off.

He went first of all to Bors House, the manor of the late Sir Timothy Bors. Sir Timothy had lived there alone, able to employ a woman to do a little cleaning only once a week, and occupying, as previously remarked, but three rooms of the huge building in whose architecture could be traced every century of taste in British building.

Bors House was one of the few moated manors left in Britain. To be sure, the moat was but a ditch whose walls had, during time, tumbled to a great extent and were covered with weeds and grass so that the moat could readily be forded by a boy. But nonetheless it was a moat, constructed to keep out besiegers and stocked at one time with marvelously large carp.

There was a rotten drawbridge over it, leading to the main gate of the manor house. This part of the building dated from the eleventh century. It had the eleventh-century massiveness to it; stones as big as sacks were used for building. The walls in this area were seven feet thick. There was a portcullis and a postern gate beside it, and this particular area of Bors House was as massive as a castle. There were three towers for bowmen over the main gate, and below the rampart connecting them, once manned by men in the livery of the owner, was the family coat of arms—a tusked boar, rampant et regardant, and beneath it the grim motto: *Deus meum fortitum creavit,* "God Made Me Strong."

This was not the oldest part of Bors House. Beyond this massive and martial gateway was a courtyard surrounded by other buildings—an armory, a buttery, a mews, a huge stable, a bakery, and at the far end of the courtyard from the gateway, a building whose walls were made of mud, stone and huge balks of timber. This, patched for thirteen hundred years, dated from the seventh century. It was this place that Sir Timothy preferred and in which he had lived.

The building had something of the appearance of a sack of potatoes. It was all slouched over on itself. The walls were not plumb and the windows were wildly askew. In parts, particularly around the bottom, the walls bulged as if pressed out by the weight above them. Further, the timbers which ran through these walls, and which had originally been pieces of twelve by twelve oak, had splits half an inch wide running through their lengths and were bent as if they were but slender planks. All looked, indeed, as if it were about to collapse. And yet this building, a remnant of its former self, still stood distorted but strong, somewhat, Cibber thought, like the British nobility.

Cibber went to the front door and was about to knock when it was opened for him.

Sir Timothy Bors stood before him. "My dear fellow," said Sir Timothy, "do come in. Where have you been, and what have you done with the rabbit?"

"You're dead," said Cibber, ignoring all this and getting to what was for him a far more important matter.

"Am I really?" said Sir Timothy, putting his hand to his face as if he had been accused of needing a shave. "Oh yes. Of course I am. That milk van. Fellow wasn't looking where he was going at all. Of course, neither was I. In fact, I couldn't see a thing. Surprisingly dark inside a suit of armor."

While he babbled on he had led Cibber into the main room of his residence, a place of large proportions but furnished in a curious manner. There were two noble carved chairs of wood, of venerable age, one on each side of a fireplace of such size that a tree trunk would have made a reasonable log for it. Facing the fireplace, in the place of a couch, was the rear seat of Sir Timothy's Rolls Royce. King Arthur was sitting on this, staring into the fireplace and taking no notice of either of them. There were three windows in the living room each with a large sill before it that was cut out of the wall. And on the sills were burlap sacks stuffed with wool to serve as cushions.

"Woolsacks, my dear fellow," said Sir Timothy, seeing Cibber eying them. "The oldest kind of cushions in the realm. There's one in the House of Lords, you know, provided for the convenience of the Lord Chancellor. Try one, or perhaps you might be more comfortable in a chair. Made by Walter the Painter, the fellow who made the Coronation Chair in Westminster. Edward III ordered three and then couldn't pay for the other two, so the family took them over in payment for beating the Scots most bloodily."

Cibber decided on one of the chairs which creaked as he lowered his weight into it.

"The King's thinking," said Sir Timothy. "I've been filling him in on the state of England, told him that Queen Maud is now our sovereign and that the Princess Pamela is the heiress apparent and everything is taken care of by the Benevolent Party these days, and so on."

"What I want to know," said Cibber, switching the topic of conversation to something which had troubled him deeply, "is why you two disappeared the other night leaving me to face Mr. Melton and the law."

"Disappeared?" said Sir Timothy. "But my dear old chap, we didn't disappear at all. Here we are, as you see."

"I bent down to pick up me ferrets," said Cibber doggedly, "and when I stood up again you was gone. That's disappearing."

"Oh, that's because we're dead," said Sir Timothy. "You see when you're dead you only have to desire to go somewhere and there you are. Space has no meaning at all, nor time either, for that matter. We overlooked the fact that you are still alive and would have to walk to the manor. By the way, how long ago was that?"

"Three days, more or less," said Cibber.

"Three days?" echoed Sir Timothy. "It only seemed like a second to me. I'm getting very vague about time already. Do you suppose you could tell me how long I've been dead? Just as a matter of curiosity."

"Three days, too," replied Cibber. "Your funeral's tomorrow."

"I shall refuse to attend," said Sir Timothy stoutly. "Wild horses wouldn't drag me to it. You've no idea how I've suffered at funerals during my lifetime. I used to have to attend the funerals of people who were absolute strangers to me—because of my position as an hereditary nobleman, of course. But the agony of it. Standing around for hours with my feet getting colder and colder and with a horrid smell of mothballs from the pallbearers' suits intermingling with the aroma of beer from the sexton who always had a glass to fortify himself. There always seems to be a nasty wind at funerals. Many a time I've envied the deceased in his nice snug coffin without a care in the world and quite safe from catching a head cold.

"No. Nothing would persuade me to attend my funeral. Absolutely nothing! I won't hear of it." He paused for a moment and then said, somewhat less fiercely, "Still, I hope there's a good turnout. It would only be respectful, you know. Where is the funeral to take place?"

"St. Cymric Thorpes," said Cibber.

"Ah," said Sir Timothy. "Very nice too. Well, I hope the weather's fine.

"But tell me," he continued, "you say it's three days since we last met, though I can scarcely credit it—what were you doing in the meantime?"

Cibber told Sir Timothy how he had been arrested for the dual offenses of poaching and illegal use of the public spade, and Sir Timothy was quite pleased at the thought that the magistrate had not been unsympathetic to the story that he, Sir Timothy, had returned from the dead. At least that was the construction he insisted on putting on it, though Cibber said the opposite had been true.

"That fellow Beauchamp is quite a sound man," he said.

"He's a Conservative and so has faith to fall back on for his lack of brains. That's the whole strength of the party. Courage, faith, goodwill, and no damn nonsense from foreigners. It has always been sufficient."

But Cibber had something other than politics on his mind and asked Sir Timothy whether he liked being dead.

"I absolutely adore it," said Sir Timothy. "If I'd had my choice, my dear fellow, I'd have been dead a long time ago. Why, the very thought of not having to fill out that wretched ten-page income tax return in itself makes death worth while. And when I think of being relieved of the necessity for going down to the government personnel bureau every month and registering myself and quarreling with that stupid clerk about whether my occupation should be listed as 'nobleman' or 'unemployed,' I positively rejoice at having passed away.

"It's the only thing these days, old man. Absolutely the only thing. You wouldn't care to join us, would you? A quick jump off the top of the main rampart and you literally wouldn't have a care in the world."

"Not me," said Cibber, who for the first time experienced a twinge of fear at being in the presence of the two spirits.

"Well, everyone to his fancy," said Sir Timothy. "I was only trying to look to your comfort as my guest. If at any time you should change your mind, please don't hesitate to ask."

"Thank you very much," said Cibber.

"Not at all," said Sir Timothy. "The fact is that I've taken rather a fancy to you—because of your poaching on my estate, you know—and I should rather like to do you a kindness."

Cibber was becoming increasingly apprehensive since it was

plain that the greatest kindness Sir Timothy could think of would be to kill him, or at least assist in arranging his death.

"I'll speak me mind plain, Sir Timothy," said Cibber. "And I've no liking for dying before my time."

"Don't give it another thought," said Sir Timothy. "I was only wishing to be helpful, as I said."

The King now stirred in his seat. Since he had, as far as Cibber could discover, been thinking for three days, he expected that Arthur would announce some great plan of procedure. But having moved as if to speak, Arthur settled back once more against the seat of the Rolls Royce and appeared to be lost in deep thought.

"I don't want to be disrespectful," said Cibber, "but I hope His Majesty will come up with something soon."

"He's only been thinking a moment," said Sir Timothy.

"A moment the way you look at it," replied Cibber, "but three days on my calendar. If he goes on like this, maybe I'd better come back next year."

"Well, he's got rather a lot to think about," said Sir Timothy. "Thinking's dreadfully hard work, you know. I was never very good at it myself. When I was alive and had to think about anything difficult, I got indigestion. You don't suppose the mind is actually situated in the stomach, do you?"

"I wouldn't know about that," replied Cibber. "I just wish the King would hurry up. It seems simple to me. He came back to help us. I don't know why he should find that hard."

"I fancy it's a matter of where to start," said Sir Timothy. "Whether to start, for instance, with you and your spade (he knows about that, of course, because he knows about everything) or the stabbing of Wat the Tyler or the Children's Crusade or the problems of Princess Pamela and Chuck Manners . . ."

"I never heard of anybody called Chuck Manners," said Cibber. He was beginning to think that Sir Timothy was not right in his mind.

"You haven't?" said Sir Timothy. "How extraordinary! Oh, but of course you haven't met him yet. How stupid of me. It's very puzzling being dead because the past and the present and the future are all mixed up together. To tell you the truth, I can't make head nor tail of it myself. Probably never will. But I'm used to being in a muddle. I was in a muddle all my life, you know. People with very few brains have just as hard a time of it as people with minds like Einstein's. What I mean is that they work just as hard, but they never get any credit for it."

He gave a somewhat pathetic, spaniel-like look at Cibber, as if at one and the same time apologizing for his lack of mental prowess but expecting fair treatment.

"You mean that we're going to meet the Princess Pamela?" asked Cibber.

"Oh dear. Oh dear. I get so confused," said Sir Timothy. "You're sure you haven't met her yet?"

"Positive," said Cibber.

"Nor Chuck Manners? He drives a truck."

"No," said Cibber.

"Well, they're somewhere around. That's all I can say."

"Never heard of him," said Cibber, doggedly.

"Probably we'll meet them when we go on the quest," said

Sir Timothy. "We're bound to go on a quest. It's an old habit of the King's, you know. He was frightfully keen on them when he was alive, like beagling and being active in the harriers."

The mention of the word "quest" distracted the King from the morass of thought, involving it seemed the whole history of England, in which he had been floundering. He looked sharply at Sir Timothy and said, "You are right, Sir Knight. We must go on a quest."

"What shall we quest for, Your Majesty?" asked Sir Timothy, bubbling with excitement and rubbing his hands together with glee.

"My sword, Excalibur," said the King. "It must be found for it holds the solution to all our problems."

Chapter Six

CIBBER had some reservations over the plan to go questing for the sword Excalibur, and they arose out of his previous experience of the King and Sir Timothy. Briefly, it would be awkward for him, a mortal, to set out with two spirits who were not, like himself, bound by time and space.

"Supposing," said Cibber, "that the two of you decided we ought to go to London. You'd be there in a jiffy and I'd still be here in Somerset having to take the bus.

"Then again there's this business of time. The King's forgotten all about time, having been dead so long. That makes it awkward. If I was to suggest that we were to meet at such and such a place tomorrow, the King doesn't know what I mean by tomorrow, and he might turn up there a thousand years from now—or even yesterday."

Much of what Cibber said made no impression on the King

who had long lost the terms of mortals and dwelt only in the timeless and spaceless dimensions of the spirits. But Sir Timothy was still sufficiently earthbound to be able to catch, in a vague manner, what Cibber was saying. He could not, however, explain the matter in detail to the King, lacking as he did terms of reference. He contented himself then with pointing out that it would be difficult, if not impossible, for a mortal to join forces with spirits and to this the King agreed.

"However, there is no great problem here," he said, "for all we have to do is kill him."

"I offered to do him in," said Sir Timothy cheerfully, "but he seems stuck on staying alive."

"That's right," said Cibber firmly.

"You pledged at our first meeting that you would be true to me even unto death," said the King sternly.

"Yes, but I didn't pledge to be true even unto suicide," said Cibber.

"I think you have a point there," said Arthur and the three fell silent.

"I have a suggestion to make," said Cibber at length. "Why don't you two become mortal again—just for a while?"

"No, thank you very much," said Sir Timothy quickly. "Your fears of death are as nothing to the dread which overwhelms me at the very thought of rebirth."

"To be confined in that lonely cell of flesh and blood and bones again," said Arthur, "is so terrible a thought that you cannot understand what you are asking. It is the only true imprisonment. The spirit is held captive in pain-filled, narrow bounds and beats against the confining walls of mortality, its every action chained to the dull and limited movements of a human frame. It cries for freedom, knowing eternal and unbounded freedom, and may not have freedom. The aches and hungers and hurts of the body, its desires and its needs, its sweating and its cold, its illnesses and its exhaustions—all these are tortures, but they are nothing as compared with the longing of the spirit to be free. You do not know what you ask. It is like asking a mortal confined sixty years in a solitary cell, in which he cannot stand, sit, lie or kneel, to return to that cell."

"It ain't that bad," said Cibber. "There's compensations. A pipe of tobacco of a fresh morning, a nice cosy fire of a frosty night, a tight roof over your head when the wind howls and the rain falls, and a glass of October ale with company. Being alive ain't as bad as you think it is. You've just forgot."

But the King only groaned at the prospect.

"Well then," said Cibber, "since you don't want to be reborn and I don't want to die, there's an end to it all and I might as well go back to ditch digging."

He got up to go, and he intended to go, but the King said, "Stay, churl. Even a King may hesitate before leaping into life. To die for your fellow men is one thing. But to accept life for them, to be born for them, that is another and more dreadful thing altogether. Yet, I will do it."

Cibber returned to the fireplace. He half-expected that the King would say some formula from an ancient book of magic by which his spirit would once again be clothed with flesh. But the King merely rose and went to the window and stood there in the beam of sunlight, looking out. He appeared to be looking upward into the sky, and yet, as Cibber watched him, it became plain that the King was looking far beyond the sky and the sun, beyond the blueness which represents infinity for mortals, into the voids which lie above and about the meager atmosphere of the earth. How Cibber knew this, he could not later explain. He just knew that it was so—that the King was communicating with an immense power, the source of all life, which lived in infinity. His lips were moving but Cibber could hear no sound. Then the glow of light which had up to that moment glimmered around the King went, as if the sun had disappeared behind a cloud, and a kind of heaviness came over the figure of Arthur. His shoulders slumped, his body seemed to twist gently, his face grimaced. He closed his eyes and bowed his head upon his chest as if in severe pain, a pain so great that he could not even cry out against it.

And then Cibber noticed a shadow form on the floor behind the King. It was but a smear of grayness to start with, but it became more and more opaque until at last it was deep and firm.

"It is done," said the King at length, raising his head. "I am once more mortal. Feel the wretched flesh on me." He held out his arm and Cibber grasped it and felt the muscle beneath his clothing.

Sir Timothy had been watching this performance from the other side of the window. Both now turned to him.

"It is your turn now," said Arthur. "Stand firmly in the light and look outward as I did to the Source."

"If you don't mind," said Sir Timothy, "I'd rather not."

"What?" cried Arthur. "You refuse?"

"I know I'm not putting up a very good show," said Sir Timothy, "but I've only had a very little time being dead, and I like it so much that it would be a hardship indeed to ask me to return to life.

"Besides," he added desperately, "I haven't been buried yet. It would be rather awkward if I turn up alive with my corpse still in the coffin. That would make two of me, one alive and one dead, and lead to all sorts of trouble. It might utterly shake people's faith in death, and unless people believe in death, they're liable to become—well, irresponsible.

"What I mean is," he continued hurriedly, "if people knew for certain that I was lying in my coffin in the church in Glastonbury, and yet I was at the same time walking around here in my own home, the effect on life insurance companies would be disastrous. And then there's death duties and inheritances, see? I mean they all depend on somebody's dying and staying dead as is expected of them. And if they started coming alive again, the legal muddle would be something appalling. Death's a very convenient thing, you know. We could hardly run life without it, if you get what I mean."

"I think he's right," said Cibber. "People know he's dead, and as he says, he ain't been decently buried yet. It wouldn't be right to resurrect him afore he's been interred. 'Twould make a terrible muddle."

"I might be able to help a little, too, by remaining in the spirit world," said Sir Timothy. "You know, scout around a bit and tell you what's going on in other places and so on."

It took considerably more argument, but finally the King agreed, though with no good grace.

"Well," said Sir Timothy at length, "that's settled. And now the thing to do is to find Excalibur. That means setting out on the quest. Nobody has the faintest idea where Excalibur is so that it doesn't really matter in which direction we head. That's the nicest thing about a quest. You just get up and go."

"On a horse," said the King. "Nobody ever went on a quest on foot. It is unseemly."

"Horses are rather difficult these days," said Sir Timothy. "They've all been nationalized under the Land Use and Horse Control Act. Or maybe it's the Horse Control and Land Use Act. One horse, under license to every ten acres of marly soil, or fifteen acres if the subsoil at the depth of six inches is chalk —and then for decorative purposes only, which has played hell with hunting. They're not to be ridden or put to work, just kept so that the children can see what a horse used to look like in a field.

"Of course," he continued, "they've got a lot of horses in the zoo, but that's in London. I have the Rolls, though. Perhaps we could use that?"

"What about petrol?" asked Cibber. "Petrol's pretty high."

"What a petty kind of start!" cried Sir Timothy, very vexed indeed. "You might as well say 'What about hay?' Can you imagine a knight mounting his horse to start upon a quest, armored at every point, carrying perhaps the glove of his lady in his helmet and his lance properly couched and then saying, 'What about hay? I wonder where I shall get hay for my horse?' Come, my dear fellow, you must develop a better spirit or you will fail from the start."

"Four shillings a gallon," said Cibber doggedly. "That's

what petrol costs these days. And if them Arabs start acting up again, it may be five and a tanner or six bob."

"Tut, tut," said Sir Timothy impatiently. "Can't you get your mind off mundane matters?"

"It's all very well for you to talk," said Cibber. "From here on everything's free for you. You don't even have to pay a penny for a night's rest. But for me and the King it's different. We're living in the world of cold cash."

"Oh dear, oh dear," cried Sir Timothy, quite exasperated. "You're spoiling everything. Here I am on the eve of my very first knightly adventure, when I expect to meet with fair maidens in distress and wizards and all kinds of exciting things, and all you can do is talk about the cost of petrol and the attitude of the Arabs toward the people of Britain. Well, if you insist upon talking about money, you'll find a hundred pounds under the woolsack there. I'd been keeping it in case of a rainy day, but I don't think it's going to rain any more where I am."

Cibber removed the woolsack in the window and, directed by Sir Timothy, found a loose stone in the window sill, which he removed, and discovered in the cavity a hundred one-pound notes.

The King was very interested in the money and took one of the bills and looked it over carefully.

"This woman," he said, pointing to the figure on the note, "looks like my sister, Morgan le Fay."

"That's Britannia," said Cibber.

" 'Bank of England Promise to pay the Bearer on demand the sum of One Pound,' " he read. "I see that it is signed with the name O'Brien. O'Brien was King of Ireland. Do the Irish now issue money to the people of England and control the treasury?"

"Oh no," cried Sir Timothy. "Matters have not come to such a pass. He's just the cashier of the Bank of England."

"It is strange," said the King, "Morgan le Fay in league with the Irish. That smells of trouble. I do not like it." He threw the note down on the window sill. "This is not money," he said. "It is nothing more than a written promise of money."

"Well, it's the same thing and serves the purpose," said Cibber.

"I shall have no need of it, churl," said Arthur. "If money is to consist of a promise in writing, then I should think the word of King Arthur is as good as that of the Bank of England."

"There you are," said Sir Timothy. "That's more like it. Why don't you put the money back? You'll have no need of it. King Arthur will issue his own notes."

"Maybe he will," said Cibber. "But people at petrol stations prefer these," and he put the hundred pounds in his trouser pocket to the disappointment of the knight.

The question of money having been settled, the King now turned to a matter which, as the founder of all chivalry, concerned him closely.

"We must arm ourselves for the quest," he said. "Sir Timothy, lead me to your armory that I may select those weapons proper to whatever adventures may lie before us."

"I have a few weapons, Sire," said Sir Timothy, "but they are not, I fear, in good repair. Yet some might serve with a little mending. Come this way." Sir Timothy immediately disappeared, to Cibber's annoyance.

"Drat him," he said. "That's just what I was afraid of. He's forgotten that he's a spirit and that we are mortals. Lucky we know where he's going or we might never find him again." Sure enough, Sir Timothy was in the armory waiting for them. He stood before a rack of ash spears, twelve of them, of which the longest were perhaps twenty feet. Arthur looked them over and selected one, as a billiard player might take a cue. He put the point on the floor and, holding the haft on his shoulder, rotated the spear, glancing along its length, and then shook his head.

"Your armorer should have turned these spears a little every day and rubbed them with neat's-foot oil mixed with a little powdered chalk," he said. "But the rogue has left them stand too long in one position and, it being damper close to the wall than in the center of the room, all are, no doubt, warped. Many a good knight has been unhorsed in a hastilude through such carelessness." He grumbled on about the spear and finally chose one of medium length which was in better condition than the rest. He then called for armor and selected a suit of light German steel which he put on, though he had first to wrap himself in an eiderdown to cushion the armor, there being no padded jupe to serve this purpose. Sir Timothy suggested that he might find it rather hot, but the King gave him a look of scorn and said that in his previous time on earth he had spent many a midsummer day in armor, fighting from sunup to sundown, pausing only occasionally on agreement to sharpen weapons and drink a cup of wine.

Cibber, meanwhile, took the spear outside and strapped it on top of the Rolls Royce and hung a piece of red cloth on the end of it as provided by the highway code. He also took the back seat of the Rolls, which had so long formed a couch for Sir Timothy, and reinstalled it in the car.

Then the three entered the Rolls. Cibber, who in his youth had served briefly as a chauffeur, took the wheel and the King and Sir Timothy sat in the back.

"Drive on, my good fellow," said Sir Timothy.

"Where to?" asked Cibber.

"Anywhere," said the knight, happily. "Anywhere at all." He leaned back in the seat, the engine gave a preliminary cough or two, and they set out on their quest.

Chapter Seven

THE PRINCESS PAMELA, younger and only sister of the childless Maud I, Queen of Great Britain, and heir to the throne, was feeling blue. To combat this feeling she should, had she taken the advice of her principal lady in waiting, Lady Beatrice, have been reading poetry, preferably some "good English poet" like Wordsworth.

"Whenever you're feeling depressed, my dear," Lady Beatrice had said to her many times, "think of the gay daffodils nodding in the breeze and read Wordsworth's poem on the subject. Then, if you take a glass of Enos Fruit Salts, you'll probably be all right in the morning. Unless it's influenza."

But Princess Pamela didn't like poetry for she had had far too much of it during her schooling, and instead was looking moodily over her collection of bus tickets. She kept the collection in a number of cigar boxes and it was without a doubt the biggest collection of its kind in England. She had started it in her childhood, stooping surreptitiously to pick up a bus ticket while the Queen was reviewing a parade, and had kept the hobby up. She had bus tickets from every city and town and county in England but she liked the London ones best. The penny tickets were white and the twopenny tickets blue and the threepenny tickets were pink. The shilling ones, which were somewhat rare, were a dull gray and reminded her of the Archbishop of Canterbury.

The Princess was a wholesome and attractive girl of eighteen, somewhat forthright in her manner, and a little too high spirited perhaps for royalty (at least that was the view of the Lady Beatrice).

Besides bus tickets she had another hobby, deliberately followed to offset too-nice an education. She was an expert on Australian slang, which she was discouraged from using around the palace, although she used it often enough with White Stick in Waiting, the officer of the Household Cavalry whose task it was to act as her bodyguard. She'd started with American slang but she found Australian somehow more satisfying and besides it was easier to learn. White Stick in Waiting had lived several years in Australia and had taught her most of what she knew. She thought he was a bit of a bunny (that is, not very bright), but he was not, like the Prime Minister, a wowser (someone who hopes to gain Heaven by frowning on other people's pleasures).

What depressed the Princess was the thought of the schedule which had been laid out for her for the following day by the

Lord Chamberlain, after consulting with the Queen and the Prime Minister.

At 8:30 in the morning she would have breakfast with her sister, Queen Maud, and the Prince Consort in the gold dining room. The Prince Consort would spend breakfast solving the *Times* crossword puzzle and the Queen would give her last-minute instructions on propriety to brace her for the day's work. Breakfast would be pretty miserable, but then it always was.

At 9:30 she would be driven to Regent's Park Zoo to open a new wing which was to be devoted to British birds.

At 10:45 she would be at the British Museum reading a prepared speech to members of the Woking Archaeological Society who were celebrating their golden jubilee. (The Princess was honorary president of the Woking Archaeological Society, she was aggravated to discover.)

At 11:45 she would have lunch in the new Ministry of Agriculture canteen, and she already knew the menu. There would be a tired salad with some kind of shredded fish from South Africa, snorkels (sausages) made from Hampshire hogs with mint sauce from Suffolk, mashed murphies grown in Norfolk and Brussels sprouts from Lancashire. She abominated Brussels sprouts which wept a thin green water into the gravy whenever served.

She was to be sure to say that she liked the shredded fish from South Africa because it was important to the South Africans. Actually she hated fish of any sort. There would also be a strong cup of tea from the British part of India which she was to say she liked, too. The British part of India planned to market it in America as PRINCESS PAM'S PICK-ME-UP.

"They take my tummy and use it for sales promotion," the Princess said savagely.

The afternoon would be taken up in a similarly tiresome manner with a visit to a children's fair at Vauxhall, tea at a factory where goloshes were made, and then a quick look at the work of young British artists being shown in a room of the National Gallery. Young British artists bored her and always had. She had, to mix a metaphor, a tin ear when it came to art, but had mastered a lot of jargon and could say that a picture had "impact" or "diffused radiance" or a "sense of conflicting space."

She had learned these phrases by heart and found that they could be applied to any picture and people liked them. *The Sunday Pictorial* had often assured its readers that Princess Pam could, were she not a Princess, make a name for herself as a connoisseur of modern painting, which the Princess assured Bunny, or White Stick in Waiting, was a dish of applesauce.

The only picture which she really liked was one in her bedroom which showed the "Charge of the Light Brigade." Everybody said it was deplorable art, but she liked it. In the forefront of a line of lancers on galloping, sweat-lathered horses, was a young Hussar officer with an interesting, foxy face. He was smoking a cigar and the Princess often wondered whether he was still smoking it when he got to the Russian guns, and whether indeed he had survived the charge.

In the evening the Princess would go to a night club with

an Italian count to offset the effect of having had to go to the same night club twice in the previous week with an Albanian duke.

Thinking over her list of appointments for the following day then, while examining her bus ticket collection, the Princess decided that she would have to pull a skinner. It was no use pretending she was sick. The appointments would merely be postponed and when she got well, they'd be waiting for her. In any case, all her days were spent in keeping similar engagements, which seemed to constitute her life's work, and she couldn't take to her bed and be sick for the rest of her life. That would be as bad as keeping the appointments.

The thing to do was to disappear—just walk out on the whole business, and not come back until she'd had a decent time by herself living the way she wanted to. For one thing, she wouldn't take breakfast at 8:30. She'd lie in bed until, perhaps, eleven or so even if it was, as Lady Beatrice said, bad for her character. (The Princess wondered idly for a moment why, in the British view, bed was regarded as bad for one's character. The French, she understood from Bunny, took quite an opposite view, holding that maturity can hardly be achieved without a considerable time spent in bed.) Another thing—if she got away on her own she'd jolly well make sure that she never went near the zoo or the British Museum or the National Gallery or any building or place in the slightest degree associated with the stuffier aspects of British living. But she'd spend a good deal of time riding buses. She had never ridden one and she wanted to ride one.

Having halfway decided to pull a skinner, indeed to do a

bunk, the Princess picked up her pile of one-and-ha'penny tickets (dark brown) and wondered whether she could enlist the services of Bunny in getting, undetected, out of the palace. That would be the hard part. A pass was needed to get in and out of the palace and all the servants had these passes. But she couldn't get in or out without the Lord Chamberlain's being informed and her sister, the Queen, and Bunny had to go with her and usually the Lady Beatrice or someone designated by her. And the thing to do, of course, was to get out alone.

The Princess put down the bus tickets and went over to the window and looked down into the palace yard. It was empty, though of course there was the usual policeman at the gates and the guards marching their beat outside the railings. As she watched, a back panel truck pulled into the yard and went around to the rear of the palace where goods for the royal household were delivered. She watched the truck for a moment and then went into her sitting room and looked it over. There was an extremely large cupboard in one corner with some complicated eighteenth-century locks on it. Locked from the outside with one handle, the cupboard could not be opened from the inside. She knew that because she had had Bunny lock her in it once just for fun and she had been unable to get out.

She rang the bell and White Stick in Waiting came into the suite of rooms. He was a tall and extremely handsome officer, but not at all like the Hussar in the "Charge of the Light Brigade." The Hussar looked ferrety and reckless but White Stick looked noble and dull.

"Bunny," said the Princess, "there's a funny little rustling noise in the back of the big cupboard, and a squeaking noise, too. It may be a mouse or a bird. You know Belham's boy" (Belham was the major-domo and had an apartment in the servants' quarters of the palace) "keeps white rats and he lost one the other day. They have pink eyes and no hair on their tails and I don't like them."

"Good Lord," said Bunny, reaching instinctively for his sword which, of course, he was not wearing.

"If it's the white rat it will be eating my shoes. And I'm afraid to go in after it. Anyway, if I found it I wouldn't know what to do. Would you go in and deal with it for me?"

"Certainly, Your Highness," said Bunny.

"Thanks, cobber," said the Princess.

"Don't mensh," replied Bunny.

He stepped into the cupboard and the Princess closed the door on him and turned the lock. Then she quickly put on a green twill raincoat and a small, green felt hat and a pair of gloves which were unfortunately white, picked up her purse which contained twenty pounds and some shillings and walked quietly out of her quarters.

She slipped along the corridor outside her apartments in the direction of the servants' wing, grateful that there was no one around for it was tea time, and entered the servants' elevator. She pressed the button for the basement, and found herself, when she left the elevator, in a large and gloomy cellar, stocked with crates and barrels and trunks and several heads of animals shot by her ancestors. There was a flight of steps leading out of the cellar and she went up these to find that she was standing at the tradesmen's entrance to the palace; that is the place where plain vans carrying supplies for the palace kitchen unloaded their goods.

No one of the staff was around. The black panel van was still there, however, the rear doors open, and standing beside it, looking at the upper story of the palace, was a young man with a butch haircut. There was about him the air of an American, betrayed both by the haircut and the stance which lacked a certain British deference.

BOOK II

The Flight of the Princess

Chapter Eight

CHUCK MANNERS had arrived in England some two years previously. His home was Santa Barbara, California, and he was a postgraduate student at the University of London, researching material for a dissertation which would give him a doctorate in English literature. He had originally intended to write his dissertation on Oliver Goldsmith, but had been sidetracked into the Arthurian legend, in much the same way that a man opening an encyclopedia in search of the word "motet" can become hopelessly ensnarled in reading about Marsupials. He had come across one fascinating and remote writer of the Arthurian story—Llydriff of Snowden, who seemed to have lived around the time of the Venerable Bede, and who therefore had been writing about the Arthurian saga before the renowned Geoffrey of Monmouth.

Chuck had become so attracted to this figure, who seemed

to beckon to him from the mists of Celtic history, that he put Goldsmith aside in search of Llydriff of Snowden. He had found several verses constituting part of a poem which could be attributed to the author, but was unsuccessful to date in finding the final verses of the poem. One verse, at least, he suspected, was missing. His original grant for study had been spent and, since his work was not yet complete, Chuck had obtained a dispensation from the British authorities which permitted him to work to earn his keep and so continue his researches.

The work he got had, of necessity, to be of an odd-job nature, and this made it difficult to find employment. British employers sought people who were going to stay with the "firm" for the rest of their working lives. They were not interested in giving a job to a young American who, however useful he might be, had no intention of remaining in their employ any longer than was necessary.

So Chuck had obtained most of his employment as a casual truck driver. He was a good driver, knew a little about mechanics, was cheerful and willing and didn't dawdle on his trips. Indeed, his current employer, Mr. James Barton of the firm of Barton and Willing, tea merchants and suppliers to the Royal Family, had once expressed the wish that Chuck would give up the study of history, become a British subject, and settle down to a solid future in the tea business.

"The tea line is not to be sneezed at," said Mr. Barton. "I flatter myself that I am a good judge of character and I fancy that you are a born tea man."

Chuck had thanked him but said that he would prefer to

continue his studies and retain his citizenship. When he had his degree he would return to the States and teach.

Because he proved so reliable and cheerful, Mr. Barton had decided that he would entrust Chuck to deliver the supplies to Buckingham Palace on that day—the regular driver being down with a cold. Such a commission, he was at pains to explain, was not normally given to men with less than ten years of service with the company.

"I'm making an exception in your case, Chuck," said Mr. Barton, "because I fancy as an American you would like to say that you have been inside the palace gates."

"Thank you, Mr. Barton," Chuck replied.

"Very historic place, the palace, as you know," continued Mr. Barton. "Not many Londoners, even, get inside the gates. Now you show your pass and drive around to the back and one of the footmen will take the tea from you and give you a receipt. We don't bill the palace of course. That's all taken care of automatically. You may be delayed a little time there, but then there'll be plenty of interest for you to see. The third window from the right on the second floor is of special interest. That's the room George III died in, so I'm told. Some say he was murdered."

"Maybe I'll see the Queen," said Chuck.

Mr. Barton gave a deprecating little laugh.

"The Queen never goes near the servants' quarters," he said. "Nor the Princess either." And then fearful that he might have sounded a little stuffy, and anxious in the way all the English are shyly anxious not to upset American visitors, he added with an attempt at jocularity, "If you see the Princess Pam, you can give her your regards from California."

"Okay," said Chuck. "You're not forgetting that I'm taking a few days off tomorrow for research?"

"No," said Mr. Barton. "I'm not forgetting."

And so Chuck Manners of Santa Barbara, California, postgraduate student at the University of London and part-time van driver, was standing in the rear of Buckingham Palace, looking up at the window of the room in which King George III was alleged to have died, when the Princess Pamela came out of the palace cellar.

Chuck spotted her immediately and for a moment could not believe what he saw. He could not believe it because, putting aside what Mr. Barton had said about the royal family never visiting the servants' quarters, he just did not think it likely that the heiress to the throne of England would be down in the palace cellar.

"Hello," he said and smiled at her and tried not to stare.

"Hello," said the Princess, somewhat shocked herself for this young man looked remarkably like the dashing Hussar who for so many years had led the Light Brigade against the Russian guns in the painting on her bedroom wall.

"Name's Chuck," he said. "Regards from California."

"California?"

"Yes. That's where I come from. The boss said that if I met the Princess Pamela I had his permission to give her regards from California."

The Princess smiled.

"Regards from Buckingham Palace," she countered.

"Thanks," said Chuck.

The Princess eyed him for a few moments.

"I suppose you know who I am?" she asked dubiously.

"Sure," said Chuck. "You're the Princess Pamela."

"I was afraid of that," said the Princess.

"Afraid of it?" Chuck asked.

"Yes. You see I don't want to be the Princess Pam. At least not for a while. I want to take a holiday."

"Well, why don't you?" asked Chuck.

"It isn't that simple. I'm thinking of running away."

"Oh," said Chuck.

"Yes," said the Princess.

"You see," said the Princess with a rush, "I really have to get away. Just for a little while. Otherwise tomorrow I have to go to the zoo and talk about British birds and then to the British Museum and talk about British Archaeology and then have to eat some South African fish and some snorkels from Hampshire at the Ministry of Agriculture canteen, and it's just too poisonous to think about so I have to drag the chain a bit."

"Drag the chain?"

"Loaf," said the Princess. "I locked Bunny—that's White Stick in Waiting (he's supposed to look after me)—in the cupboard and I thought maybe you'd help me go walkabout."

"Go walkabout?" repeated Chuck.

"Yes," said the Princess with a touch of impatience. "Don't you talk English? Hide. I have to get out of the palace grounds and I thought maybe you'd let me go out in the back of your van—that is, if the Americans are really as friendly as they say they are."

This was a most unfair advantage for the Princess to take of Chuck and she knew it. But she was a ruthless young lady when it came to getting her own way, and she made the cut without even as much as a blush. As for Chuck he felt on the moment that the honor of the United States was immediately at stake. Here was a lady in distress appealing to him as an American, and as an American it was up to him to help her. Furthermore, she seemed like a nice kid and he wasn't going to pass up the possibility of a private interview with the heir to the throne of England.

He did not however accede immediately. "What had you got in mind?" he asked.

"Very simple," said the Princess. "Just let me get in the back of the van, drive me out say to Trafalgar Square, and let me off there."

"And then what?"

"Well, then I'm on my own."

Chuck was momentarily appalled at the prospect of what he was about to agree to. If it were discovered that he had helped the Princess out of the palace, he would be in deep trouble both with the British government and his own government. He didn't know what the penalties would be but he would probably be expelled from England, putting an end to his research into Llydriff of Snowden.

"No," he said, "I can't do it."

But the Princess, while he was thinking, had sidled over to the back of the van and now jumped inside.

"Can't do it," said Chuck reaching to get her out.

"Too late now," said the Princess and slammed the doors shut, nearly catching his fingers in them.

At that moment a footman emerged from the kitchen with the receipt for the small chest of tea which Chuck had delivered. He signed the receipt and the footman withdrew.

"Come on out of there," Chuck hissed to the Princess when they were alone.

But she had locked the doors on the inside (the van was provided with such locks for the safety of anyone required to ride in the back), and he was rewarded only with an off-key rendering of the American National Anthem. He rattled the door but without avail, and another footman appeared and asked him if he were having any trouble. "No," said Chuck and, since the man continued standing there watching him suspiciously, he got into the van and drove off.

With what he now regarded as a "hot" Princess in the back of his van, Chuck was at a loss where to drive to, or what to do next. He contemplated for a moment going to the United States Embassy in Grosvenor Square and turning the Princess over to the American authorities who might be expected to stand by him as an American citizen. But then he reflected that it might be exceedingly embarrassing to the embassy to have him dump the Princess on them. He had by now driven through St. James's Park to Trafalgar Square and the Princess was hammering on the partition which separated the driver's compartment from the rear of the van.

What he could do, he reflected, was just stop the van in

Trafalgar Square and let her out, and he slowed down to do this when a policeman appeared and waved him on.

He turned down Whitehall, but when he slowed down again once more a policeman appeared. Furthermore, there were a great number of people around. The Princess was extremely popular and well-known and he was panicky at the thought of having her get out of the back of his van in the sight of such a multitude.

It occurred to him that what he should do was drive out of London altogether, somewhere on the Great West Road, and there release the Princess, in some sparsely populated area.

And so he drove out through Kensington and Hammersmith until he picked up the Great West Road and came at length to Staines. When he had gone through the town he pulled up a side road, stopped the engine, got out and called to the princess to dismount.

"You're a pig," said the Princess when she had opened the doors. "Why didn't you let me off in London? I've broken the heel of my shoe hammering for you to stop."

"Look," said Chuck, "I didn't invite you into the van in the first place. So now out you get and on your way."

"I'll do nothing of the sort," said the Princess. She picked up her handbag, opened it, took out a mirror and, still sitting on the floor of the van, repaired her make-up.

"When I said that you are a pig," she said between applying a touch of lipstick, "I didn't really mean it."

"What did you mean?" asked Chuck.

"I only meant that you're not very cooperative," and she

removed the mirror from before her face and gave him a smile full of sweetness. "Where are we?" she asked.

"Just outside Staines," said Chuck.

"Wonderful," said the Princess. "And what are we going to do next?"

"What do you mean what are *we* going to do next?" demanded Chuck. "*We're* not going to do anything. You're going to get out of this van and I'm going back to London and forget all about you."

"You're not very smart, are you?" said the Princess. "I always heard that you Americans were smart, but you're acting like a twit."

"A what?"

"A twit. A simpleton. If you'd let me out in London as I wanted you to, you could have got away with it. But you can't get away with it now."

"Get away with what?" asked Chuck.

"Kidnaping me," said the Princess calmly.

"Kidnaping you!" cried Chuck. "But I didn't kidnap you. You got into the back of my van and you wouldn't get out."

"And so you had to drive me all the way to Staines?" said the Princess sweetly. "Against my will?" she added. "That's kidnaping. I can prove that because I broke the heel off my shoe struggling to get out of the van. I expect you'll get life for it—in the Tower."

"Listen," said Chuck fiercely, "this is a frame-up, and you know it."

"Certainly I know it," said the Princess. "Of course it's not altogether a frame-up. I did get into the van and lock myself in. But it was your idea to drive me out here. So I repeat, what are we going to do now?"

"I know what *I'm* going to do," said Chuck. "I'm going to drive to the nearest police station and hand you over. That's what I should have done before."

"Very cold in the Tower," said the Princess meditatively. "Lots of rats too. In the old days they used to put people in wells with rats in them and the rats nibbled on them and it was very unpleasant. Of course, I don't suppose they do that now. There have been *some* improvements. Still, the Tower isn't the kind of place I'd like to spend twenty years of my life."

Chuck groaned. "Okay," he said. "You win. What do you suggest?"

"Well," said the Princess, "what were you going to do if you hadn't kidnaped me?"

"I *didn't* kidnap you," said Chuck fiercely.

"A mere technicality," said the Princess. "Skip it. What were you going to do? Something interesting, I hope."

"Well," said Chuck. "I was going to pick up my old car and caravan and go down to Somerset for a week and prowl around down there—Glastonbury mostly."

"Prowl around doing what?"

"Oh, I'm looking for Celtic material. You wouldn't understand. Llydriff of Snowden."

"Sounds horrible," said the Princess. "But I'll come."

"You'll what?"

"I'll come. It would be nice to get out into the country and picnic and camp and so on. Where is your caravan?"

"In a garage in Chiswick."

"Well, let's go and get it."

"No," said Chuck stoutly.

"You're not being very gallant," said the Princess.

"Look," said Chuck. "Couldn't you just be a sport and go away and leave me alone? I mean I haven't done you any harm, and you're going to get me into a jam sticking round. Couldn't you just take a bus or something and sneak back into the palace and forget all about this running away?"

"No," said the Princess. "I've been to considerable trouble to get out and I'm not going to sneak back in again, even if it were possible. In any case they'd want to know how I got out in the first place and there you'd be—on the spot."

"Couldn't you just give them some kind of a story and get me off the hook?" pleaded Chuck.

"I could," said the Princess, "but I wouldn't. I'm out and I'm jolly well going to make the best of it. In fact, I may never go back. So we might as well go and get your caravan and start our adventure. Unless you want me to turn you over to the police?"

"Turn *me* over to the police?" gasped Chuck.

"Yes," said the Princess. "For kidnaping me."

Chuck now realized that he was completely in her hands, and her hands were not very scrupulous.

"Look kid," he said, "you've got me over a barrel. So I have to play ball with you. But do me one favor will you? Cut off your hair. It's a dead giveaway. Everybody knows your hairstyle. How about it?"

"Righto," said the Princess. "I never liked it anyway. It's

not my idea but was thought up by the British Hairdressers Association. They're sneaky. They thought up the most expensive way of dressing hair and then had me dress mine that way, and now everybody has to spend a lot of money fixing their hair if they want to be fashionable. I'd have cut it off long ago if I had had a chance."

There was a pair of scissors, not very sharp, in the cubbyhole of the van. They were there to cut strings on parcels if needed and Chuck got them. He got into the back of the van with the Princess and sat her upon a box and took a handful of her soft hair and started cutting. He wasn't very good and he wasn't helped by the fact that the Princess kept moving her head. He had hoped to achieve a short bob, but kept getting the ends uneven and he finally wound up with a haircut which looked not unlike that of a man though longer. It completely changed the Princess' appearance so that he was amazed at the difference it made in her.

When they had done this they drove back to Chiswick and picked up Chuck's car, an A-Model Ford, and an old caravan. Chuck paid an apprentice at the garage a pound to take the van and drive it to the London yard of Barton and Willing, tea merchants.

The Princess borrowed some stationery at the garage (she had a very winning way with her), wrote a short note, put it in an envelope, borrowed a stamp, and asked the apprentice to mail it when he got to London. He promised he would do this.

The two then left and stopped at an Army and Navy Store to pick up some clothing for the trip. Then they drove away along the Great West Road toward Glastonbury.

Chapter Nine

"TELL ME," said the Princess Pamela, licking some butter off the tips of her pink fingers, "do you suppose that you were ever at the Battle of Balaklava?"

It was the afternoon of the following day. They had camped for the night at Windsor Park and were now having a picnic tea on the roadside just outside of Frome.

"Balaklava?" said Chuck. "That was fought before the Civil War. I'm only twenty-two."

"I'm twenty-one," said the Princess. "I seem to have seen you somewhere before."

"Probably when you visited London University," said Chuck. "I was the five-hundredth man on about the fourth row to the right. I was eating an ice cream."

"I didn't notice," said the Princess. "I was trying to remember the name of the Chancellor—of the university, that is. If it wasn't Balaklava it must have been somewhere else."

"It must have been somewhere else that what?"

"That I met you before. I seem to have a sort of residual memory of you. A nice memory," she added archly.

"Look," said Chuck, "I expect being cooped up in that palace and surrounded by flunkies didn't do much to improve your wits. But we couldn't have met at the Battle of Balaklava, because the Battle of Balaklava was fought in 1854 and this happens to be 1972. And we weren't either of us born, and I wish you'd just get a train and go back to the palace and let me go on my way."

"Well, if it wasn't Balaklava it was somewhere else," said the Princess ignoring the suggestion, "because I'm sure that we've met."

"Like I said," Chuck replied, "in the quadrangle of London University. There were five hundred people and an ice-cream cone between us, but my personality charmed you immediately. Do you mind telling me what you propose to do when this little adventure of ours is over? Not that I want to be nosy. I'd just like to get an inkling of what's in store for me."

"Always thinking of yourself," said the Princess. "Well, I might decide to go to America—incognito, of course. Tell me, what's it like in California?"

"Swell," said Chuck. "Sunshine every day of the year, oranges bursting out of people's back yards. Beaches. Mountain and lake resorts. All the tourist stuff. And no princesses."

"If it's as nice as all that," said the Princess, not a whit disturbed at the thrust over princesses, "I wonder why you came to England?"

"Had an appointment with Llydriff of Snowden," said Chuck, "King Arthur and so on. I'm preparing a dissertation on the Arthurian legend and ran into old Llydriff and I'm trying to chase him down. There are some pieces missing."

At this point a car swept down the road past them and the Princess gave a scream and said, "Did you see what I saw?"

"No," said Chuck who had been intent upon getting the last of the sugar out of his teacup. "What did you see?"

"A Rolls Royce driven by a man in full armor," cried the Princess. "Quick! Let's catch it!"

She hurried into the Ford. Chuck got behind the wheel and

they chugged off in the direction taken by the Rolls. They had not far to go. They drove but half a mile down a side road and found the Rolls Royce in a ditch with an armored man standing beside it and another man, unarmored, shaking his fist at him.

"I told you you couldn't drive," said the unarmored man, who was, of course, Cibber Brown. "But you're so stubborn you had to find out for yourself."

"My breastplate is bent and my greaves started," complained the man in armor. "Fetch an armorer, for I cannot go questing in this plight. Also fetch that invention of the devil out of the ditch. It is bewitched."

"Isn't it hot in there?" asked Chuck, addressing himself to the King and eying his armor.

"Of what degree are you, caitiff?" demanded the King, lifting his visor and glaring at him.

"Master of Arts, UCLA," said Chuck. "What are you doing in the armor?"

"I am Arthur, King of Britain for all time," replied the King.

"Concussion," said Chuck to the Princess. "You know, some of the daffiest people in the world live in England," he added pointedly.

"Where is Sir Timothy?" demanded the King of Cibber.

"I don't know," said Cibber. "He probably got out when you took the wheel, scared out of his life, even though he is dead already." A horrible thought crossed his mind. "You didn't do this to kill me, did you, hoping to free me of being alive?" he asked.

"I have already given you my word, churl," said the King, "that you will not be harmed in that way unless you specifically desire it of me, when I will grant you the boon of death."

"We'd better get out of here," said Chuck. "I think this guy's off his rocker."

But the Princess was intrigued. The man in armor had said he was King Arthur and she certainly wasn't just going to turn her back on someone who made such a claim.

"Did I hear you right?" she asked. "Did you say you are King Arthur—Arthur of the Round Table?"

"I am, my lady," replied the King.

"This is one for the book," said Chuck. An idea occurred to him and he turned to the Princess.

"Pinch me," he said.

"Why?" asked the Princess.

"Never mind. Just pinch me. Hard." She did so and he said, "Ouch."

"If he is possessed," said the King who had been watching this performance, "the malevolent spirits may sometimes be driven out by pinching or driving pins into the flesh. But hot irons on the feet, since they are reminiscent of the fires of Hell, are more effective." He now looked narrowly at Chuck and said, "We have met before, you and I."

"Balaklava," said Chuck. "I was one of the horses."

"Hey," said Cibber, "how about helping me out of the ditch here?"

"Okay," said Chuck who had decided to roll with the punches for the time being. He asked Cibber to help him unhitch the caravan. When this had been done he backed the

Ford to the rear end of the Rolls, produced a piece of chain and linked the two cars together with this. King Arthur and the Princess meanwhile sat side by side on the top of a nearby bank watching them.

"I'm worried about Sir Timothy Bors," said the King, while the Ford tugged like a bulldog at the heavy Rolls.

"Who's Sir Timothy Bors?" asked the Princess.

The King told her about Sir Timothy and explained that, being now a spirit, he had lost all sense of time and place and might have difficulty finding them again. She was so surprised by the explanation that she could think of no comment to make on it.

"I think the churl was right," the King continued, "and Sir Timothy got out of that engine when I made it plain that I intended to drive it. He is not used to being dead and sometimes gets confused and still thinks that he's alive and might get hurt."

"Did he know where you were going?" the Princess asked.

"Yes," replied the King. "Camelot. We agreed on it shortly after setting out."

"But there's no such place as Camelot any longer," said the Princess, sure now that Chuck was right and that she was in the company of a lunatic, though a very interesting one.

"I will know the place when I get to it," said the King. "It lies hereabouts. I traveled these lands hundreds of times on horseback and afoot and in carts before my death. They are greatly changed and yet in some ways they are not changed at all. The trees are largely gone—trees whose branches interlaced, so closely did they grow, that they cut off the sky.

Wonderful trees they were—beech and elm and pine and especially yews. The bracken below grew as high as a horse's head.

"The forests stretched mile upon mile between the hills. There were many lakes thick with tasseled bulrushes near their edges and with iris and marigolds growing about. Wild fowl rose in clouds from these lakes when one approached; banners of heron, both blue and white, of duck and gray geese and teal swarming up into the skies. In the forests were the big red deer and wolves and bear and lions and wild boar, lynx, dragons, wyverns and griffins and unicorns.

"All that is gone now. Yet the shape of the land, beneath its clothing of forest and water, remains. And I know that shape well, for as I say, I rode it many times.

"Camelot we built upon a hill. The hill lay in the center of a lake, and over this we had built a causeway a mile long upon which four knights could ride abreast. Beyond the lake was the Forest Sauvage through which there were but small roads.

"When riding through these forests my knights carried their swords before them, the hilt making a cross to summon God and his saints to their aid against the forces of evil."

The Princess sighed. "Those must have been wonderful days," she said. "Everything is so dull now." The King made no reply.

After a little while he said, "What are you doing upon the road with this young fellow?"

"If I tell you will you promise not to reveal anything to the others?" the Princess asked.

The King nodded agreement and the Princess told him who she was and how she had come to run away from the palace.

When she had finished, the King said nothing. He just looked grave and the Princess could not tell what caused this and was afraid to ask.

Chapter Ten

IT TOOK THE better part of an hour to get the Rolls out of the ditch and the King, after the first twenty minutes, got tired of sitting on the bank and went over to supervise the task. Since he had no understanding at all of the functions of automobiles and believed that they operated through some will of their own (which was the reason for the accident), he was not of any great use immediately. He formed the opinion now that some kind of spell had been cast over the Rolls and that was the reason that it had sped down the road as soon as he was seated behind the wheel and had crashed into the ditch.

"I did nothing more than put my foot upon the ground," he said to the Princess, "when it speeded up and flew away with me. Undoubtedly some kind of an enchantment has been worked upon it."

"You probably had your foot on the accelerator," said the Princess.

"It would not surprise me if this were the work of Merlin," said the King, ignoring what for him was an utterly nonsensical explanation. "He has great power to move things. As for instance, he moved all the stones which form Stonehenge over from Ireland in a single night. Then he moved the castle of Tintagel three miles, so that an army set upon besieging the castle could not find it and perished dolorously in the wilds of Cornwall."

"When you put your foot on the accelerator," said the Princess patiently, "the car speeds up."

"If Merlin has done this," continued the King, "then there is no sense striving to undo his work. Only he can withdraw the spell. Though Sir Emeryss of Lyonesse, whose mother was a witch so that his brothers and sisters were all either black cats or wild dogs, told me once of a way of abating these enchantments."

"What you should have done was take your foot off the accelerator and put it gently on the brake," the Princess said firmly.

The King turned to her sternly. "I am older than you and know more about these things," he said. "I don't think you are listening to me."

"But you don't understand about motorcars," said the Princess. "You see, they're man-made machines and so men can control them. There is no need for spells."

"Tell me," said the King, "do these machines always work well?"

"Properly treated, yes," said the Princess.

"Even properly treated they never stop working?"

"Well—hardly ever."

"And what then?" asked the King.

"You call a mechanic and he finds out what is the trouble."

"Always? Without fail?"

"Well—almost always."

"But sometimes he does not find out the cause why the machine stopped, or behaved in a strange manner?"

"Yes . . . That's true. Sometimes he can't find out."

"Well, that is when an enchantment has been put upon it by Merlin," said the King. "Sorcery was not abolished by these strange inventions. I suppose nobody blesses these machines before venturing out in them?"

"No," replied the Princess.

"Ah," said the King, "it is most dangerous and lacking in Grace not to call on God's blessing before starting upon a journey. One of my knights once set out upon a quest to Gaul in a little boat. And although he was himself blessed by a hermit before stepping in the boat, he neglected to obtain a blessing for the boat itself. He was hardly gone from the shore before the boat was seized by a powerful spell cast by a wizard and whisked up into the air, and there he remained for twenty-three years until by prayer and fasting he had obtained the forgiveness of God for his sin of omission."

"I should have thought he would have starved to death long before that," said the Princess.

"Those whom God wishes to punish," said the King simply, "He can readily keep alive for twenty-three years without food. I find that you are lacking in faith, but it is a fault of the young, for when one is young one thinks one can find answers to everything. It is only when you are old that you realize that reason is the poorest of faculties and little reliance can be placed upon it, and therefore faith is essential unless you are to be overtaken by melancholy and madness."

By now the Rolls had been wrestled back onto the road by Chuck and Cibber. But it was just as well off in the ditch for neither of them could get it started. They tried all the usual remedies but without avail, and then lifted up the hood and checked the spark plugs and the fuel pump and the lead from the coil to the distributor, but their efforts went unrewarded.

"I am trying to recall, while we wait for Merlin, what it was that the knight said," said the King.

"You mean the one that was up in the air in the boat?" asked the Princess.

"No. I mean Sir Emeryss of Lyonesse whose sisters were all black cats. He told me how to abate these enchantments. Let me see." He pondered for a while and then said:

> "Bud of suckle, flower of dill,
> Haw of rose about to fill,
> Henswort, cowbane, stem and root . . ."

He paused.

"What rimes with root?" he asked.

"Boot," said the Princess brightly.

"Dilligrout," said the King. "That's it.

> "Bud of suckle, flower of dill,
> Haw of rose about to fill,
> Henswort, cowbane, stem and root,
> Heat all well for dilligrout.

"A murrain on it!" he exploded. "All I've remembered is a recipe."

"It sounds very interesting," said the Princess. "What's dilligrout?"

"It's a soup served at coronation banquets," said the King. "It tastes like hot mud. Plague blue its bones. I thought I had hit on the counterspell. Well, I'll have to try again. Let me see now:

> "Crabbed apple, nut of Spain
> Ear of wheat . . .

"No. That's a poultice for spear thrusts through the left side. The one for spear thrusts on the right side is the reverse —nut of Spain, apple crabbed, and so on. I must keep trying." He remained for some time in deep mental struggle and then shouted, "I've got it! Here it is!

> "Switch of hazel, twig of beech,
> Spring of ousel, one of each
> Bound together, serve as leach."

The two of them gathered the pieces of wood from the trees mentioned in the jingle and the King bound them together with a tie of grass.

"We must put these upon the proper place," said the King.

"That bunch of twigs?" said Chuck scornfully. "Just what good do you think that will do?"

"Just what good have you done, my friend?" asked the King gently. He gave the twigs to Cibber who put them on the distributor.

"It will work now," said the King. "I have the information from the son of a witch, dead now fifteen hundred years."

Cibber got behind the wheel and pressed the starter. The engine fired up immediately.

"Wait a minute," said Chuck. "Open up that top again. This doesn't make sense." The top was opened and Chuck put his hand on the bunch of twigs and withdrew it swiftly and danced around, shaking his hand for he had received a potent shock. The princess laughed deliciously.

"You Americans," she said. "Always trying to find explanations for things. Can't you just be satisfied when something works and leave it alone?"

"It's a short," said Chuck. "That's all."

"It is a counterspell," said the King calmly. "No man should set out on an adventure, particularly in such an engine as this, without memorizing several of them."

"Nuts," said Chuck still shaking his hand.

"Merlin will be here soon, I fancy," said the King. "He will probably be disguised. He prefers to travel in disguise since he is a wizard. Be courteous to all you meet upon the road for when he is angry he can be very dangerous."

"Now I've heard everything," said Chuck and got into the Ford. But whatever mechanical ailment the Rolls Royce had suffered from, now seemed to have transferred itself to the humbler car, for it refused to start. Again Chuck and Cibber went through the tedious job of checking the ignition system, but when Cibber suggested that they get pieces of hazel, beech and willow and put them on the distributor cap, Chuck would have none of it.

He strongly suspected that he was the victim of some elaborate English legpull, and the fault in the ignition of the Rolls had been slyly fixed by Cibber who then pretended that the remedy lay in the bunch of twigs. He suspected too that someone had tampered with the Ford in some manner which he could not immediately discover. So he spent some more time checking the electrical circuit from the battery forward, but all to no avail.

"What we ought to do," said Cibber at length, "is hitch the caravan to the Rolls and leave the Ford here. We can send a mechanic out when we get to the next village, and by that time the spell may have worn off."

"Spell, baloney!" said Chuck, but he finally agreed. The caravan was hitched to the Rolls and Cibber and the King sat in front and Chuck and the Princess in the back and they went on their way. Cibber drove slowly at the King's request— in low gear at hardly more than ten miles an hour. This gave the King an opportunity to inspect the countryside through which they were passing closely and reconstruct it as it had been during his previous time on earth.

"We must be nearing Camelot," said the King, "for we have passed over three hills and three valleys, and on each of these three hills there is a windmill."

"I haven't seen any windmills," said Chuck.

"That is because they were pulled down a thousand years ago," said the King. "You can only see in the present time, but I can see in past time and present at the same moment.

"You see over there to the right a long meadow and I see it too. But I also see in that meadow a host of people of every degree upon their knees. In the middle of them is a scaffold, and standing on it a man clad in the tattered robes of a hermit.

"His name is Peter and he is telling the people that they must send their children in a crusade to Palestine to rescue the Holy Sepulcher from the hands of the infidel, for only the innocent and pure of heart can achieve such a high and noble purpose.

"The parents will send their children, much as they love them, to follow the hermit, and the children will die of hunger and of thirst and of torture and many of them will be sold into slavery. But there is no way to prevent it, for it has all happened.

"So it has always been when men try to shape with their hands the will of God."

"Do you see nothing good in the fields?" the Princess asked.

"I see the grass growing and the sun warming the earth," said the King.

When they had gone about four miles on their way, they met a Royal Automobile Club patrolman, riding a motorcycle with a sidecar containing tools and parts. He was dressed in the familiar blue uniform of the famous automobile club, and spotting the RAC badge on the front of the Rolls Royce, he saluted courteously.

"Stop," said the King to Cibber, "for this may be Merlin."

Cibber stopped and the King got out of the car. It is possible that the patrolman may not have seen the King properly when he was still in the Rolls. He might therefore have been expected to show some surprise when the armored figure got out of the car. But either the training of RAC patrolmen is such that they have complete control over their emotions, or the patrolman was accustomed to people in fourteenth-century armor getting out of ancient Rolls Royces.

Whatever the explanation, he showed no surprise at all, but having put his motorcycle to the side of the road, he came over to them and said, addressing Arthur, "Having any trouble, sir?"

"We were," said Chuck. "Somebody jinxed the engine."

The RAC man looked at Chuck without the shadow of a smile.

"Sometimes they do get jinxed," he said. "Mind if I have a look?"

They opened the hood once more and the RAC man immediately spotted the bundle of twigs which was still lying (though this was surprising) on top of the distributor cap.

"I don't think we'll be needing those any more," he said quite seriously and threw the twigs away. He then took the cap off the distributor, examined it and the points but did nothing to adjust them, merely putting the cap back. He looked at the coil and the spark-plug leads and the fuel pump, just feeling the connections with his fingers, and then said, "I think she'll start now."

Cibber pressed the starter and the engine fired up dutifully.

The Princess had been studying the face of the RAC man closely. It was an impassive face, weather-worn and brown, with wrinkles around the eyes and the corners of the mouth, and she could not tell from looking at him whether he was forty or sixty or maybe fourteen hundred years old. Once, during the examination, his eyes looked into hers, coolly and appraisingly, and the Princess felt sure that he knew all about her, not only all about her past but all about her future.

When he removed the twigs she had noticed a slight smile on his face, nothing more than the movement of the muscles at the corner of his mouth. What kind of a smile was it? she wondered. Was it the smile of an expert automobile mechanic at sight of a completely ridiculous remedy for engine trouble? Or was it perhaps a smile of recognition; a smile indicating that he had known that the twigs would be there and he was a little pleased that Arthur, his student as a boy, had remembered this remedy?

"Anything more I can do for you before I disappear?" asked the patrolman, and the choice of the word "disappear" startled the Princess.

Was it possible that he would disappear? And was it possible that he had appeared? She had not been looking at the road ahead when the patrolman came in sight on his motorcycle so she could never be sure on that point.

"My Ford's stalled about five miles back," said Chuck. "Maybe you could fix it."

The patrolman thought a minute, looking Chuck over carefully. "Would you care to come back with me to it?" he asked.

"Sure," said Chuck. "I don't want to leave it by the side of the road."

He got out and the patrolman indicated that he should sit on the top of the sidecar.

"How far is it to Camelot?" asked the King. The Princess heard the question distinctly, though she was not sure the patrolman had heard it for he had just started his motorcycle and the noise might have drowned out some of the words.

"Two miles," the patrolman called out. "Straight ahead. You can't miss it. You'll recognize it by a sign which says Witham Friary."

Chapter Eleven

THERE ARE NO inns or hotels or even boarding houses in the hamlet of Witham Friary. It is a place about which very little is known, though situated in a populous island, and it is a paradox of modern travel that more Englishmen know Rome or Lisbon or New York than know Witham Friary, which is situated in their own island and less than a hundred miles from their capital.

There are, of course, thousands of such places in England and indeed in every country of the world. They lie down the backroads, not only of topography and of geography but of history. No event of any mark has ever happened in any of them. No kings or presidents are ever born in them. They are the scenes of no great stroke in human affairs. If, by chance, a man or woman of some note is born in such a place, they seem to leave it early and, upon achieving prominence, never refer to the place of their birth. And so these places remain in their isolation, though surrounded by a bustling and pushing world, largely untouched by the events of the nation as a whole, by the forward sweep of history and technology, browsing gently, as it were, in the fields of Time, waiting for nothing, aiming towards nothing, and on the whole remarkably content with their lot.

Witham Friary looms larger upon the map than it does upon the land. The very name itself on the map gives it a prominence which its physical appearance does not justify. For it consists of nothing more than two or three cottages and a convent. In the eleventh century there had been an abbey upon the site which continued, with varying fortunes, until the dissolution of abbeys and monasteries under Henry VIII. Then, the nuns having been ejected, the building was taken over and turned into a wool factory where weavers (mostly Flemings encouraged to migrate) not only worked at their trade but, likewise, lived and raised their families. But the factory did not prosper. It was, for one thing, too remote from London, which put up the cost of the finished goods. For another, it was difficult to keep the weavers together in one place. They migrated to London themselves. And finally the factory was abandoned, and the old empty abbey stood, unused except as a shelter for sheep and cows, for three hundred years, its stones being plundered one by one for the building of cottages and walls, until there was but the empty shell of one transept left.

Then, following the relaxation of the laws against freedom of worship, a group of Catholic nuns had arrived from France, bought the site for a small sum, and with the remaining stones, built a convent at which to carry on the charitable work of caring for and educating orphans. Children were sent to them from various charitable organizations and the sisters took them in, scrubbed them, clothed them, fed them, educated them and, when they had reached the age of sixteen, found some employment for them in the world outside.

Arthur, whose vision was not merely of the present but of the past, saw the convent on its little knoll and saw also the great abbey which had preceded it; saw the tonsored monks singing the splendid Mass in Latin; and saw further than that the castle-city of Camelot itself, which Merlin had built, with around it the silver lake and the noble causeway crossing over its surface, and on the borders of the lake, the huge trees upon whose tops the eagles nested and looked as small as sparrows.

He saw a hundred bright pennons streaming from every pointed tower of Camelot, saw the rich tapestries hung from every window to be aired—silver damask, cloth of gold, black velvet worked in turquoise thread—sensed the rich old accustomed smell of horse sweat and leather, and the sharp burned aroma of shod hoofs striking sparks from flint roads, and seeing and sensing all these things, he ordered Cibber to stop the car while he dismounted.

"I will rest here awhile," he said. "Do you go forward into Camelot and tell them the King has returned and to prepare for him."

Cibber was by no means anxious to perform this mission.

"I don't want to be disrespectful," he said, "but they'll think I am out of my mind unless you come with me—"

"Churl," said the King sternly, "did you not promise to serve me even unto death?"

"Yes," said Cibber.

"Then go to Camelot and tell them I am coming and to prepare for me."

"We'd better go," said the Princess.

"You'll come with me?" asked Cibber.

"Of course."

"Well, we'll leave the spear with him. I expect he'd like that," said Cibber. In truth, however, he wanted to be rid of both the spear and sword, thinking these strange baggage with which to turn up at a convent in a Rolls Royce and request a a night's lodging.

They therefore put the spear beside the King, who had withdrawn a thousand years or so from them, and drove off to the convent. They found a large door in an alcove at the front of the convent; a door studded with iron bolts and with hinges on it sufficient to withstand the attentions of a battering ram for some time, and rang a bell which hung outside.

After a little while the door was opened by a nun who looked at them rather fearfully for a moment and then relaxed.

"Oh," she said, "I thought you were the building inspector. Is there anything I can do for you?"

"Can you give us lodging for the night?" asked Cibber.

The nun looked beyond them to the Rolls Royce with the caravan hitched to it. The Princess guessed what she was thinking and said, "We are not really asking for ourselves, but for someone else."

"Who is that?" asked the nun.

"King Arthur," said the Princess.

For a moment the look on the face of the nun was one of astonishment. But it immediately softened into a look of compassion.

"Can you wait a moment while I talk to Reverend Mother?" she asked and went away, leaving the door half-open. She was back in a while and now her attitude was one of warm concern.

"Reverend Mother said it would be quite all right to bring the gentleman here," she said. "We will take care of him. Where is he now?"

"We left him about two hundred yards down the road. He told us to come here—that is, to Camelot—and announce his arrival."

"Of course," said the nun soothingly and with great understanding. "He will be welcome and we will do all we can for him."

When they got back to the King, they were surprised to find that he was sitting upon a plough horse which had been grazing in a roadside field, and the horse was standing upon a slight rise in the center of the field. The King had his lance at rest, that is to say horizontal in front of him, and the visor of his helmet was open. The horse had, of course, been nationalized and had on its flank the cipher BCH 224 FVO which meant British Cart Horse No. 224, For Viewing Only.

"Sometimes I don't think he's in his right mind," said Cibber confidingly to the Princess. "He gets mixed up over what century he's in. I don't know whether he can handle twentieth-century problems with a sixth-century mind."

The King seemed to have read these thoughts of Cibber's, for as the two approached, he said, "You are wrong to doubt me, churl. You look askance at me astride this charger upon a hilltop so that I may be seen from afar outlined against the sky. Yet when a man takes a stand upon some matter, if the matter be worthy, such is the position he should take—upon a hilltop where all may see him and know that he is there to defend the right against all comers. And this is as true for the twentieth century as for the sixth century and for all the time that men shall be upon the earth. And he who will not stand forth as champion of those truths in which he believes is a knave and a coward and undeserving either of the company or the respect of his fellows.

"Am I awaited at Camelot?" he continued without waiting for comment.

"Yes," said the Princess.

"I will take the horse," said the King. "I may have need of him."

"That'll make trouble," said Cibber.

But the King paid no attention and, touching his heel to the animal's flanks, he took off at a hand gallop for the convent on the nationalized cart horse, thereby violating a number of ordinances. The others returned to the car and arrived at the convent as the King was dismounting.

The door was opened by the same nun, but she had with her, in the corridor, what amounted to a reception committee of nuns, among them the head of the house, Reverend Mother Gabriel. Reverend Mother was elderly. She had a cheap but stout walking stick with which to support her ancient limbs.

Her face was like a wrinkled apple but her eyes were those of a child—untroubled and innocent.

When he had dismounted, the King removed his casque which he gave to Cibber Brown and also unbuckled his sword and gave this also to Cibber. Then he walked forward to where Reverend Mother Gabriel was standing a little to the side of the other nuns, and kneeling before her, asked her blessing, identifying himself as King Arthur and asking whether there was any right which he might defend for her or any wrong which he might set right on her behalf. This brought a rustle of whispering among the nuns which Reverend Mother, venerable though she was, silenced by rapping her stick upon the hardwood floor.

"You are the first man in all England who has offered to defend us," she said. "How strange that is. But you must be hungry and tired, so let us give you what we have to offer and then you must rest yourself well."

Cibber was told where he could stable the horse, and the three ate supper with the nuns and were shown to separate rooms for the night.

Meanwhile Chuck and the RAC man had found the Ford. To Chuck's annoyance it fired up immediately the latter had pressed the self-starter and idled admirably with the dogged chug-hiss-chug-hiss-chug common to A-Models.

"I don't understand it," said Chuck. "It wouldn't start at all half an hour ago."

"Sometimes it takes a special touch, sir," said the RAC man. "But I don't think you'll have any more trouble." He

paused a moment and then said, "Would you mind if I in-quired where you are from, sir?"

"Santa Barbara, California," replied Chuck. "I'm over here preparing a dissertation on the Arthurian legend."

"That should come pretty easy to you, sir," said the RAC man.

"Why?" asked Chuck.

"If you were to think about it, sir," said the other seating himself on the saddle of his motor bike, "I have no doubt you could remember a lot that you've forgotten." With that he started up the engine and departed with a wave of his hand, leaving Chuck very puzzled indeed.

Alone Chuck sat on the running board of the Ford and said to himself, "What I ought to do is drop this whole Arthur busi-ness and write a paper on the mysteriousness of the English. They're a nation in disguise. They present one front to the public in order to deceive everybody about what really goes on inside. It's a kind of a national tradition or maybe it's a religion. Maybe it's something they inherited from the druids —a cult of mystery that they never got rid of.

"Take that guy in the suit of armor," he continued. "He no doubt goes to his office every day wearing a bowler hat and striped pants or something of the sort, but he's always had a yen to drive his old Rolls Royce wearing a suit of armor. Maybe for a bet. Maybe because he wants to. Anyway, nobody in any other country in the world would ever do such a thing. It could only happen in England where everybody pretends to be so normal and so self-effacing and so anxious to avoid notice. And then one of them suddenly does something like that.

"You know something," he said to a linnet which paused for a moment on the hedge opposite him with a flutter of lemon-yellow and pale brown feathers, "I kind of like it. Anyone who will do something like that is worth knowing. Reminds me of California. Only in California there'd be a press agent and searchlights and television cameras and it would turn out that the guy was advertising somebody's hardware store."

The linnet cocked its small head to one side and then started busily cleaning the feathers under its wings.

What had the RAC man meant by saying that it would be pretty easy for Chuck to write his dissertation if he were to think about it, for he would remember a lot? Did he mean that he would remember a lot of things he had forgotten about Arthur during his two years of study? Or did he mean that he would remember something that . . . something that what?

"Aw nuts!" said Chuck. "It's like that crazy Princess asking me if I was ever at the Battle of Balaklava. It's just part of the English cult of mystery. They've got druids in their hair. You ask a guy what he sees in a field and he sees Peter the Hermit and the Children's Crusade. You ask a guy in California what he sees in a field and he says a million-dollar housing tract just as soon as they can get it subdivided."

His thoughts now turned to the Princess and his own predicament as the man who, it would be alleged, had kidnaped her.

And suddenly he realized that he was in the clear.

The Princess had gone off with the man in the suit of armor who called himself, for his own reason, King Arthur.

All he, Chuck, had to do was climb in the Ford and disappear. He could do even better than that. He could drive to London, withdraw all the money from his bank, buy a ticket to the States and forget about the whole thing. The British government would have a hard time pinning anything on him once he was back in the States, and even if they did he'd have a chance to tell his own side of the story.

"Brother," he said, "why didn't I think of this before?"

He climbed into the Ford and turned it around in the road, and then something else occurred to him and he switched off the engine and started to think once more.

Supposing the guy in the armor really wasn't in his right mind? Supposing he was a lunatic? Could he really leave this English girl in the hands of a lunatic?

"Sure I could," said Chuck and turned on the ignition. "Serve her right." But he then turned it off again.

"She isn't a bad kid," he said. "She's spoiled that's all. But I don't think I can leave her. Not as an American. I don't care anything about her as herself—as a girl. They got coeds at UCLA that she couldn't hold a candle to. But as an American I just can't leave her. It isn't what an American should do. It isn't what we're noted for—leaving people on the spot and just disappearing. What I mean is that I wouldn't like her to think of Americans like that.

"Aw heck," he concluded. "I guess I'd better go back and take care of her. Not that she'd do anything for me. No sir! What's going to happen to little old Chuck is that he's going to wind up in the Tower of London with rats nibbling on him. If my family had a motto it would be 'Here comes a sucker.' "

He started the engine once more and turned the Ford around and drove off. As he did so he noted a minor commotion in

the top branches of a nearby oak tree and was mildly curious about what had caused it, for there was no wind to make a similar disturbance in adjacent trees.

"Stout lad," said Sir Timothy Bors who had leaped into the top of the tree when he saw the Rolls was headed for the ditch and had remained there ever since. "Stout lad, indeed. What a pity he wasn't the one who ran over me."

Sir Timothy got down from the oak by the delightful process of merely wishing himself upon the ground.

"Let's see now," he said to himself. "I ought to join the King, and the King said he was going to Camelot. And all I have to do is wish to be there and I shall be there. Excellent. I wish myself in Camelot."

He immediately found himself on a small island surrounded by a large lake. There was a causeway across the lake to the island, upon which four horsemen could ride abreast, and indeed four horsemen were riding abreast across it. They were in full armor and on the shield of one was a wyvern gules, rampant in a field of azure; and on the shield of the second, a camelopard, couchant et regardant, sable on a field barre; and on the shield of the third, three goshawks vert, on a field argent; and on the shield of the fourth, a mandrake, volant on a field or.

All this seemed quite right and natural to Sir Timothy. As the four horsemen approached he hailed the nearest, "Gramercy, Sir Knight," he said. "I pray you take me to the King."

The four reined in and eyed him closely. Sir Timothy was of course clad in full armor, since that was what he had died in, and his shield showed the boar's head of the de Bors.

"From whence are you, Sir Knight?" asked one of them.

"Glastonbury," replied Sir Timothy.

"That lies beyond the Forest Sauvage," said the horseman to the others. "Let us seize him quickly for he is without a doubt an enemy of the King and knows where the King is held and by what magic he was taken from Camelot."

So the horsemen seized Sir Timothy and took him into Camelot where he was put in a dungeon and left there to think things over, which he was not very good at.

BOOK III

The Finding of Excalibur

Chapter Twelve

BUNNY, or rather, White Stick in Waiting to give him his official title, spent a most uncomfortable couple of hours in the Princess Pam's cupboard before he obtained his release. The cupboard had extremely heavy doors but was luckily ventilated at the top. But, because of the soundness of its construction, and also because of the size of the room in which it was situated, all the hammering he did brought no one to his immediate rescue. He was freed only when the Lady Beatrice entered the Princess' chambers to tell her it was time to prepare for dinner.

She did not find the Princess but heard a few muffled thumps coming from the cupboard and for a moment thought that the Princess had, in some manner, managed to lock herself in the cupboard. She opened the door and out fell the exhausted Bunny.

"Whatever were you doing in there?" demanded the Lady Beatrice.

"Looking for mice," said Bunny wearily.

He explained how under this pretext he had been enticed into the cupboard and had had the door locked on him by the Princess Pamela.

"Where is she now?" demanded the Lady Beatrice.

"I don't know," said White Stick. "I've been two hours in the cupboard here."

"Young man," said the Lady Beatrice, "if anything has happened to the Princess, it will be the worse for you. You were suppose to be guarding her, not acting as a mouse catcher. I will raise the alarm."

The Lady Beatrice's method of raising the alarm was to step out into the corridor carrying a small hand bell which she tinkled a couple of times delicately. Then she returned to the Princess' living room. In less than five minutes Belham, the major-domo, appeared.

"You rang, your ladyship?" he asked.

"I did," replied the Lady Beatrice. "The Princess is not in her room. Pray inform the principal servants and have them visit the various rooms of the palace in which the Princess might be and request her to return and prepare for dinner."

"Very good, your ladyship," replied Belham and withdrew. He himself went to the servants' hall and there also rang a little bell which summoned two footmen. Having communicated his mission to them, these went, one to the first-floor hall, and the second to the second-floor hall, and also rang little bells, summoning other footmen who were told what was wanted, so that soon the whole of the palace was tinkling with the sound of little bells.

Then the search began. The Blue Room, the Gold Room, the South African Room, the Canada Room—indeed all the rooms not set aside for private usage of particular members of the royal family were then visited by differing degrees of footmen who swept quietly through them, peeking into chairs and behind chairs looking for the Princess. But all to no avail. The lower footmen reported to the upper footmen, who reported to the principal footmen, who reported to the major-domo that the Princess Pamela did not appear to be in any of the rooms where she might reasonably be expected to be.

This individual conveyed the news to the Lady Beatrice, who received it with the aplomb which Wellington displayed when informed that Blücher was likely to be a bit late at Waterloo.

"Very good," she said, and dismissed the major-domo.

She went then to the apartments of the Queen and her consort. The Queen was reading a book and the Prince Consort was making another attempt on the *Times* crossword, which had defeated him since breakfast.

"Your Majesty," said the Lady Beatrice, "the Princess is not in her rooms and, although we have searched the palace, we are unable to find her."

She related how White Stick in Waiting had been locked in the cupboard and gave the details of the rooms searched. Another search was immediately ordered. It produced nothing. The palace chamberlain, having been informed, conducted a third search but with no result. The Prime Minister was called and the Archbishop of Canterbury.

The Prime Minister immediately called the High Commissioner of Scotland Yard, Sir John Menderdip, and agreed to meet him at the palace. They met, consulted, interviewed the servants, interviewed White Stick in Waiting, upbraided him jointly and separately for dereliction of duty, and the palace was searched again, this time including the cellars and the attic. But no clue to the Princess' whereabouts was discovered.

Now began a search, not merely of rooms but of cupboards and chests and barrels, trunks and indeed any kind of a container which might provide a hiding place for the high-spirited Princess. This went on until midnight when it became quite clear that the Princess was not in the palace at all.

Somebody suggested the roof and so the roof was searched, but nothing was found on it beyond the remnants of a model airplane which had disappeared after being flown out of one of the top windows by the son of the major-domo, who, it will be recalled, also kept white rats. It was returned to the major-domo with a warning against flying toy airplanes out of the palace windows.

A council was held in the Queen's apartments at which the High Commissioner, the Prime Minister, the Archbishop of Canterbury, the Prince Consort and, of course, the Queen were present.

It was plain that the Princess had gone. The question was where had she gone to, and had she gone willingly or had she been kidnaped.

The Prime Minister favored the kidnap theory.

"There are certain powers," he said solemnly, "who would stop at nothing to obtain possession of certain secrets of Her Majesty's Government in the field, particularly of thermo-nuclear rocket propulsion. We are well ahead in this field and plan to send two monkeys to Venus by the end of the year. They would of course be British monkeys. The blow to the prestige of these certain powers would be enormous. They may well have obtained possession of the Princess in order to wrest these secrets from us."

The High Commissioner pooh-poohed this theory.

"I do not see that any nation is going to kidnap a Princess just to stop us putting two monkeys on Venus," he said.

"And what, pray, is your theory?" asked the PM.

"The Princess is still somewhere in the palace."

"But the palace has been searched five times already."

"To conduct a proper search of a building as large as this," said the High Commissioner, "would take a week at least. I am not going to agree with you at all that the building has been searched. That it has been given a cursory look through is the most I will say. But it is perfectly possible, in a building as large as this, for a person to slip from room to room almost indefinitely while a search was going on and still avoid capture.

"To properly search the building, several men must be stationed in each room in the palace and in each corridor. They must be completely trustworthy. And then a party of searchers must move methodically through the building from cellar to attic looking in every nook and cranny. Only then would I agree that the building has been searched and that the Princess is not in it.

"She is, I understand, a high-spirited girl, and it is not beyond reason that she may have obtained the aid of several members of the staff in hiding her as part of a prank which she wished to play.

"My advice is for everybody to turn in for what remains of the night and see if the Princess does not present herself by the morning."

There was indeed nothing much more that could be done, and so this advice was followed.

The following morning, the Prime Minister, having first called the palace and been told that the Princess had not turned up, went to his office at No. 10 Downing Street. He had some urgent business to attend to there and he did not want, by calling immediately at the palace, to give any hint either to the public or the press that there was a crisis in the affairs of the nation.

He, therefore, seated himself at his desk and attended to the more important questions which demanded his attention, and inquired of his secretary whether there were any urgent communications for him.

He was told that there were none, though a somewhat unusual letter had arrived addressed to him.

"Unusual letter?" echoed the Prime Minister, his mind immediately busy with his kidnap theory. "Where is it, pray?"

"Here, sir," said the secretary and produced an envelope. The Prime Minister took the letter, waved his secretary out of the room, and opened the envelope. The letter read:

To the Right Honorable Prime Minister to Her Majesty, Queen Maud I:

DEAR SIR:

I have recently been thinking a great deal about my job and I do not like the working conditions, nor the hours of work, nor the prospects which lie ahead of me. I have no complaints to make about the salary and the quarters, but the hours are more than I can stand, as is also the restriction on my personal life entailed by the position. I have, therefore, decided to hand in my resignation effective as of today, and I trust that you will be able to find someone more suited to the work to replace me.

Yours respectfully,
PAMELA WINDSOR

The Prime Minister read the letter through twice, his heart pounding, unable, because of the excess of emotion, to get very much sense out of it. Then he put the letter down and walked around his desk to look out of the window into the small garden at the back of Number 10 Downing Street.

Things there seemed to be normal.

A thrush, having made a meal of a snail, was cleaning off his beak briskly with one claw, an eye cocked in case another snail might be hidden in the geranium beds. The one tree in the garden was standing upright. The grass was green and it was neatly trimmed. All he could see was firm and natural. Reassured, the Prime Minister returned to his desk, polished his glasses, gave a slight cough and picked up the letter again and read it once more.

The contents were still the same. He threw the letter on the desk in front of him and leaned heavily back in his chair and decided that he was confronted with a case of insanity. Either he had gone mad or Princess Pamela had gone mad.

He walked over to the window again and looked out. The thrush had gone, but the tree was still there and so were the grass and the geranium beds. He then left his office and went down the hall to pick up his hat, coat and umbrella and walked briskly over to Scotland Yard.

At Scotland Yard, which was but a few steps away, the Prime Minister was immediately admitted to the High Commissioner and, without as much as the formality of wishing the High Commissioner good day, he put the letter before him and said:

"Read that!"

The Commissioner read the letter and his immediate reaction was to puff out his cheeks, emitting a large quantity of air through his compressed lips and producing a hissing noise indicative of enormous official surprise.

"She must be found," said the Prime Minister. "And that immediately. Furthermore nobody must know that she ran away. Nobody. There has been altogether too much defection among royalty in recent years. It is beginning to look as if being a member of the royal family is about the least popular job we have in this kingdom. If we are to continue as a kingdom that idea must be thoroughly squashed."

The Commissioner nodded. "Tell me," he said, "was Princess Pamela in love with anyone to your knowledge?"

"No," snapped the Prime Minister. "That was absolutely ruled out in the interests of the state. A year ago she showed some kind of affection—I would not call it love—just a personal interest, in Captain the Honorable James Facel who was an equerry at the palace. He was immediately transferred to our consulate in Kabul, Afghanistan. There has been no communication between them since."

"Nobody else?" asked the Commissioner.

"Eighteen months previously she wrote a personal birthday card to young John Blennington of the Guards. Blennington was sent to our consulate in some other remote part—Kansas City, if I recall rightly—where he was encouraged to marry the daughter of a wealthy American automobile dealer. You can rule out romance altogether. She has been permitted none."

The Commissioner nodded.

"The first thing to do," he said, "will be to get a list of all the vehicles of any sort that entered or left the palace yard yesterday. I think we can rule out any possibility of the Princess having left on foot because she would have been seen and stopped."

"I can readily supply you with a list of all the vehicles which entered and left the palace," said the Prime Minister. "A note is made of them all."

"Excellent," said the High Commissioner. "I will have every one of them found and checked."

"Meanwhile, I will take this letter to the Queen," said the PM and left.

Chapter Thirteen

IT WAS READILY established that five closed vans had called at Buckingham Palace on the day of the Princess' flight and, in addition to these, three limousines. The limousines were soon cleared of suspicion. One had been that of the Archbishop of Canterbury, another that of the United States Ambassador who had been invited for tea with the Queen and her consort, and the third was that of the Prime Minister himself.

The High Commissioner then turned his attention to the five closed vans and sent five inspectors to trace them and inquire closely into what had been their errand, at what time they had arrived at the palace, and what time they had left, whether they had stopped anywhere on leaving the palace, whether the driver was well known to his employer and whether (this, of course, being the most important point) any of the vans had taken out a passenger from the palace.

The first two vans were readily cleared of suspicion. One had carried a load of clothing being returned by the cleaner whose company had been cleaning the royal clothing for fifty years. The second had conveyed to the palace fifty dozen assorted roses and the firm had been supplying seasonal flowers for the palace for a quarter of a century.

But there was a flurry of excitement over the third van. This, it seemed, had brought to the palace one hundred copies of "Come Back to Erin" arranged for the male voice, to be delivered to the Colonel of the Irish Guards regiment.

The inspector who had been sent to investigate this particular van, excited by the recurring agitations of the Irish Republican Army, immediately suspected a plot on the part of the IRA to capture the Princess and hold her to ransom—her ransom being, of course, the return of the six counties of Northern Ireland to the Irish Republic. He called the High Commissioner on the special and secret line allotted to him, and relayed his suspicions.

"The Princess may have been taken to Belfast," he said.

"Dublin," snarled the High Commissioner. "Belfast is a British city."

"I beg your pardon, sir, Dublin," said the inspector.

"Who sent these copies of 'Come Back to Erin'?" asked the High Commissioner.

"An American by the name of Michael O'Brien," said the inspector. "He hired the van with instructions to deliver the music. He may be an IRA agent."

"Well, get hold of him and ask him to come down to the Yard for questioning. If he refuses, report back. And meanwhile, keep him under close observation. I'll contact our man in Belfast."

"You mean Dublin," suggested the inspector.

"No, dammit, I mean Belfast. Dublin is an *Irish* city." With that he hung up, and then decided he ought to call the Prime Minister. He got him without delay, reported the suspicion of his inspector that the IRA might be involved in the disappearance of the Princess and might have forced her to write the note of resignation under threat of death—the note itself, of course, being a piece of propaganda to bring the British monarchy into disrepute.

The Prime Minister, who, after a night of insufficient sleep, had been trying to catch a nap when the High Commissioner's phone call awoke him, was in an angry mood. He sent a request to the Foreign Office to call on the Consul for the Republic of Ireland, acquaint him of the incident, and say that Her Majesty's Government wished to protest in the strongest terms attempts, thinly disguised, by the Government of Ireland to seduce members of Her Majesty's Forces from their duty. He could, of course, mention nothing about the Princess at this point.

The Irish Consul listened to this rebuke, and then replied that the Government of the Republic of Ireland had many times tried to raise the question of the illegal enlistment of Irish citizens in the British Army, but all this was tied up with the infamous Treaty of 1921 and the equally infamous question of Partition. He hoped that Her Majesty's Government was now willing to open up the whole question of Partition, over which the people of the Republic of Ireland had shown the greatest tolerance and forbearance for over sixty years.

The Foreign Office envoy said he had no instructions on the subject of the Treaty of 1921.

The consul then asked him whether he would like a drink and the envoy replied that he rather thought he would. They had a whiskey and soda together and discussed the pike fishing in Lough Corrib and parted amicably.

Meanwhile, the inspector who had raised the hare of the IRA went to the Cumberland Hotel where the American Michael O'Brien who had sent the suspicious copies of "Come Back to Erin" to the Irish Guards was living, and learned that Mr. O'Brien had departed for the United States. The inspector found the airline and flight number and checked that Mr. O'Brien had indeed left for the United States. These facts he reported to the High Commissioner.

The driver of the van and his employer were then brought to Scotland Yard for questioning and both affirmed again and again that nobody had been allowed to enter the van in the palace yard. The driver said that he had taken the copies of "Come Back to Erin" to the palace in the belief that the Irish Guards were stationed there, but had been informed that their barracks were at Knightsbridge, and so had left the palace and delivered the music to the Knightsbridge barracks.

It now seemed that this was a red herring, and the High Commissioner called the Prime Minister to report that the IRA might not be responsible after all for the disappearance of the Princess, but he intended to follow this lead in any case.

(He had actually contacted his opposite numbers in both Belfast and Liverpool with the result that nineteen youths suspected of membership in the Irish Republican Army had been rounded up. All of them, it seemed, were familiar with both the words and music of "Come Back to Erin" and were therefore held on suspicion of intent to cause a disturbance. They were released after twenty-four hours since no formal charge could be brought against them. Each harangued his captors, upon being released, on the brutality of the British occupation of the six counties of Northern Ireland.)

There were still two other vans to be dealt with and the High Commissioner turned wearily to these.

One had contained a koala bear sent by the City of Brisbane, Australia, to the Princess Pam. The bear had been rerouted to the Regent's Park Zoo.

The fifth van had delivered two pounds of orange pekoe tea to the palace kitchen. The delivery was a regular one and there was no circumstance attaching to it to arouse immediate suspicions.

The inspector who had been assigned to inquire into this van interviewed Mr. Barton of the firm of Barton and Willing and there turned up some surprising information. The first item was that the van had not been brought back during the company's regular hours of business. It had been returned to the company yard late in the evening, presumably by the driver.

The second item was that the driver of the van was a young American student who had a permit to work in London to help finance his studies. His name was Chuck Manners. He worked part time for the company and was now on a vacation doing some research. Mr. Barton did not know where.

The inspector got Chuck's address and questioned his land-lady only to be informed that Chuck had not slept in his room the previous night. He also made inquiries at the University of London and learned that Chuck had not attended any classes for two days.

This particular inspector was of a more phlegmatic type than the one who had jumped at the possibility of the IRA having captured the Princess Pam. He did not therefore report these findings immediately to the Commissioner, but first decided to interview the police constable who had been on duty at the time Chuck's van had arrived at and left the palace yard.

"Do you recall this particular van leaving?" the inspector asked when he had located the constable.

"Yes sir, I do," the constable replied. "Fresh young chap driving it, if you don't mind my saying so," he added.

The inspector ignored this for the moment.

"Did you search the van on leaving?" he asked.

"No, sir, I didn't," replied the constable.

"And why not?"

"Well, sir, there was a corporal's guard of the Green Howards due to pass through the gate at that moment, and I didn't fancy they'd appreciate being 'eld up while I searched this 'ere van. But I did stop the van for a moment and asked the driver if 'e 'ad anyone in the back."

"And what was his reply?" asked the inspector.

" 'E said not to tell a soul but 'e'd got Princess Pamela in there wiv the crown jewels and they was going to run off and be married. So I told 'im to be more respectful or I'd run 'im in."

The inspector blanched but still retained control of himself.

"Does it occur to you that he *might* have had Princess Pamela in the back?" he demanded.

"No, sir," said the constable stoutly, "to tell you the truth, it don't. And if anyone was to tell me that the Princess *was* in the back of that there van, begging your pardon, sir, I'd say they was barmy."

"That will do, constable," said the inspector and dismissed him. He then made his report to the High Commissioner.

"Well," said the High Commissioner when he had done, "it seems that this particular van may well have been the means by which the Princess got out of the palace unobserved. No other offers. And that opens a whole host of questions. Is this fellow, Chuck Manners, a member of the Irish Republican Army? Is he in the pay of some other foreign power with designs on the Princess? There must have been some previous correspondence between him and the Princess. It is unthinkable that she should elect to leave the palace casually in the back of a van driven by someone she had never known.

"Ignoring the international aspects for the moment and turning to . . . er . . . ahem . . . romance. Is it possible that this fellow Manners was in the employ of one of the Princess' former . . . ahem . . . suitors?

"Better check on that fellow Facel. See if he's still in Afghanistan. And that other fellow Blennington of the Guards who was sent to Kansas City. He's supposed to have married over there but people do get divorces these days. Be discreet about this checking incidentally. We don't want to arouse any speculations."

"Yes, sir," said the inspector.

"Very good," said the Commissioner with a nod of dismissal.

When he was alone, the Commissioner locked the door of his office and picked up the telephone and informed his secretary that he was not to be disturbed except for calls of the greatest urgency. He then settled down to wrestle alone with the problem of the Princess' disappearance.

Was this a case of kidnap or was this a case of the Princess' voluntarily leaving the palace as the result of some whim of her own? he asked himself.

He had made a copy of her letter of resignation and now read it through again.

"I have recently been thinking a great deal about my job and I do not like the working conditions, nor the hours of work, nor the prospects which lie ahead of me," the letter ran. "I have no complaints to make about salary and the quarters, but the hours are more than I can stand, as is also the restriction on my personal life entailed by the position." And then came the final paragraph in which the Princess tendered her resignation with the hope that someone more suitable to the position might be found.

It seemed reasonable enough—the kind of letter a young girl might write who wanted to resign her position. The point was that the position being resigned was that of heir to the throne of England and it was insane to think of the heir to the throne of England resigning with such a letter.

Or was it? Didn't that very much depend upon the personality of the heir to the throne of England?

All right. If the authenticity of the letter depended on the personality of the writer, what was the personality of the Princess Pamela?

The Commissioner, who had seen her only at a distance, attempted to reconstruct her character from the many tidbits which had been reported to him by those who had close contact with the Princess at the palace.

She was high spirited, too high spirited for royalty. This from her mother and from the Lady Beatrice. She collected bus tickets.

Bus tickets!

"Why in the name of God would a British princess collect bus tickets?" he demanded of the wall.

She was fondest of her collection of London bus tickets. The High Commissioner experienced at this juncture a slight tickling at the end of his nose, which was a sure indication to him that he was on the track of something important though what this might be he could not grasp for the moment. It was something to do with bus tickets. He must come back to that later.

All right. What else did she collect? Well, she liked cheap beads and glass paperweights of the kind sold at Woolworth's. The tickle in the end of the High Commissioner's nose diminished, so he hastily abandoned this line of thought.

Anything more?

Yes (and the tickling started again with such vigor that he was compelled to sneeze).

"Damnation," roared the High Commissioner, "I was just about to think of something and I sneezed it clean out of my head. Where was I?" He thought back to bus tickets (slight tickle), glass paperweights (no tickle), and then slang. Yes, that was it.

The Princess was a keen student of slang, particularly Australian slang. She spoke slang a great deal with the young officer whom she called Bunny (the tickling was mounting in intensity). So plainly she had gone to Australia. (The tickling immediately subsided to the High Commissioner's chagrin.)

All right. She hadn't gone to Australia. The High Commissioner almost apologized to his nose for having made such a ridiculous assumption. But it was something to do with bus tickets and slang.

Why would anyone want to collect bus tickets? Anyone could get all the bus tickets they wanted. People bought them on a bus and threw them away when used. So what was so precious about bus tickets when you could get one any time you wanted? What made bus tickets so attractive to the Princess . . .

"I've got it," cried the Commissioner, leaping from his chair and sneezing several times. "She wanted to ride a bus and be like everyone else. That's where the slang came in too." He grabbed the phone, sneezing violently.

"Have every bus in London searched for Princess Pamela," he shouted into it. "She's riding on one of them."

Chapter Fourteen

THE TASK OF searching all the buses in operation on the streets of London, not merely for one day but during the night and through the following day and night as well (for this was the duration of the search), proved far more formidable than the High Commissioner had anticipated.

The very mathematics of the task made it perhaps the most difficult hunt ever undertaken by Scotland Yard. There are, for instance, several hundred buses in operation in London, traversing several score routes. Each one of these buses makes perhaps a hundred or more stops from outset to terminus, not counting traffic stops and voluntary stops on the part of the driver who decides to pick up a passenger. Each of these stops, of course, represents an opportunity for someone to get on or off a particular bus. Added to which, the buses of London are double-deckers, meaning that a watch had to be kept on passengers going upstairs as well as those seating themselves in the lower deck. Standing is of course permitted on the lower deck, and during the rush hours all buses are crammed with passengers, many of whom invade the small platform at the back assigned to the conductor.

Given these figures and their necessary multiplication, the size of the task which Scotland Yard now undertook may be partially pictured. But there were even graver complications. First there was the fact that the Yard had not sufficient personnel to man every bus with a minimum of two detectives— one for upstairs and one for down.

Detectives from the Metropolitan Police Force and the Westminster Police had then to be called in, and these had to be supplemented by detectives from outlying towns. Still there was hardly sufficient to go around and, the news spreading through the London underworld that the coppers had taken to riding the buses and were away from their normal duties, there was a spate of crimes for the period of the hunt over the whole of the greater London area. The record shows twenty-four holdups of various stores, sixteen cases of jewelers' windows being smashed and valuable display pieces being grabbed, and five cases of bank robberies.

Since the detectives employed in the search for the Princess could not be let in on the news that the Princess had resigned her job, they were told only to seek and follow anyone whom they suspected to be masquerading as the Princess Pamela— that is, anyone who had made themselves to look so like the Princess Pamela that they might be mistaken for her. The idea behind this piece of minor deceit was to create the impression that someone was indeed masquerading illegally as the Princess, thus covering up the Princess' flight.

The results were disastrous. It turned out that at least sixty percent of London girls between the ages of sixteen and twenty-four were ardent imitators of the Princess Pamela. They wore their hair in the style affected by the Princess, wore the same kinds of hats and the same kind of make-up and arranged their eyebrows in the same manner and slavishly copied the clothing styles of the heir to the throne.

Indeed, it soon became apparent to the distracted High Commissioner that there were at least half a million Princess Pamelas riding the buses of London at all hours of the day and night. The detectives had all been instructed that when they spotted someone who might be masquerading as the Princess they were to get into conversation with her and by one means or another establish what was her true identity and obtain both her address and telephone number.

(The High Commissioner was firmly convinced that the Princess would, of course, be using an assumed name and from this arose the need for obtaining the address and telephone number of suspects.)

Several detectives were arrested by police as a result of their efforts to obtain the names and addresses and telephone numbers of pretty girls riding on the buses of London. Six, who had mislaid their official identification, or thought it indiscreet to show their credentials, were charged with "creating a nuisance" and fined sums ranging from five shillings to three pounds and given severe warnings by the magistrates concerned.

There were a great number of complaints both to the police and the press at the molesting of young girls on the London buses by what were described as gangs of adult delinquents working in partnership, and several London MPs raised the matter in Parliament.

To make matters even more unpleasant for the long-suffering detectives (who it must be admitted stuck manfully to their duty), quite a number of conductors on the buses were, of course, women. The detectives had, perforce, to question those of the female conductors who had Princess Pam hairdos, and several of them were put off buses as a result of these advances.

After two days and two nights, the High Commissioner had to call off the bus hunt. He had learned fully something of which he had previously been vaguely aware—that anyone wanted by the police in London may hide indefinitely by the simple process of riding buses and changing from one bus to another at frequent intervals.

Defeated by a superabundance of Princess Pamelas, he now conceived the theory that the Princess might have obtained some employment in London. What kind of employment? He reasoned that she would not likely take a job in an office where a growing familiarity with her fellow employees might lead to her secret being uncovered. The likeliest kind of job for her would be as a shop assistant in some extremely busy shop where the customers paid little or no attention to the girls waiting on them.

This brought about a search of every Woolworth's and Marks and Spencer store in London. These were invaded by hosts of detectives, prowling around looking for shop assistants masquerading as the Princess Pamela. The results were as disappointing as the great bus hunt. It seemed that every shop assistant had a desire to look like the Princess and once more detectives were hauled off by policemen on the complaint of the managers of various stores that their salesladies were being asked for their names, addresses and telephone numbers by strange men.

The High Commissioner had, of course, working with the Customs Department, instituted a watch on all ports and airports to prevent the Princess' leaving the country, if that was her plan. Here his task was somewhat easier for there was an automatic check through passports. He was reasonably certain then that the Princess was somewhere in England, and he now turned desperately to the Prime Minister, it being a full week since the Princess disappeared, and suggested to him that the news of her disappearance should be made public.

But the Prime Minister would not hear of it and had the support of the Queen and her consort in his stand.

"What reason for her disappearance could we give?" he asked. "We cannot announce that she dislikes her job and has resigned. We cannot say that she has been kidnaped because we do not know that she has been kidnaped. I cannot go before the public with an announcement that the Princess has disappeared without assigning some reason for her disappearance. Nothing but national chaos would result from such an action. She must be found and the news of her leaving the palace must never be allowed out."

"Well, I've tried everything I can think of and without any result," said the High Commissioner.

"Then think of something else," snapped the Premier. "What about automobiles? Isn't it possible that she had some accomplice with a car who picked her up when she had left the palace in the van and took her to some previously determined and remote spot?"

The end of the High Commissioner's nose commenced to tickle and he turned to checking automobiles.

Chapter Fifteen

WHEN THEY had been a couple of days at the convent, Chuck suggested to the Princess that they ought to move on to Glastonbury. "That's what we set out to do, you know," he said. "In any case I don't like you hanging around this Arthur guy. He seems harmless but you can never tell."

"I've been thinking about you," said the Princess. "You need help."

"Don't tell me that your stony little heart has melted and you've decided to change your plans about sending me to the Tower for the rest of my life," said Chuck.

"Oh no," said the Princess. "I don't mean help in that way. I mean that you're too serious. You're quite a disappointment as an American. I thought you'd be vivacious and play a guitar. What I mean by help is to try and get you out of yourself. Have you ever been psychoanalyzed?"

"No," said Chuck.

"Well, maybe you ought to be," said the Princess.

The two were helping in the hayfield at the convent, raking the hay together, and the remark about being psychoanalyzed annoyed Chuck.

"Listen," said Chuck, "there isn't anything wrong with me beyond wanting to complete my research, get my dissertation written and go back to California and teach."

The Princess sighed.

"I wish I could come with you," she said. "I know I'd like it in California. We could be married and I'd see that you wore the right kind of tie to impress the faculty."

"We could be what?" demanded Chuck.

"Married," said the Princess. "M-A-R-R-I-E-D," she spelled and then she flung her hayrake on the ground and ran away across the meadow to a grove of trees at the lower end, which grew by a river marking the boundary of the convent grounds.

Chuck watched her go in surprise and then turned to raking the hay again. Then it occurred to him that this wasn't what he should be doing at this particular time so he went after her. He found her sitting on the bank of the river with her feet in the water.

"Go away," she said without turning around. "I don't want to talk to you again. Ever. Now go away."

"No," said Chuck.

He sat down, laboriously took off his boots, removed his socks and put them in the boots and then put his feet in the water also. The river was deliciously cool and he gave a little gasp of pleasure. The Princess reached over and picked up one of his socks and threw it in the river.

"There," she said heatedly, "that's the trouble with you. You'd never think of throwing one of your socks in the river.

You put them carefully into your shoes and then put your big old feet into the river and sit down and grunt ... like a ... like a stupid old Indian."

"To tell you the truth," said Chuck, "people in my country don't usually throw away their socks when bathing their feet."

"I don't want to talk to you," said the Princess. "Of all the wretched luck," she continued heatedly. "I run away from the palace in the back of a van and it has to be driven by the dullest man in the United States."

"I'm sorry I bore you," said Chuck.

"You don't bore me at all," said the Princess. "As far as I'm concerned, you're just not there. Or rather you *are* there, but you're a kind of impediment in what might otherwise be an interesting landscape."

"Okay," said Chuck, "if you want I'll remove the impediment. But just remember that I didn't want you to come with me in the first place."

"That's what so hateful about you," said the Princess. "You treat me as if I was a piece of chutty that you'd stepped on and couldn't get rid of."

"Chutty?" repeated Chuck.

"Chewing gum," snapped the Princess. "If only you'd get your nose out of those old poems you might learn to speak English. I think Bunny even was more fun than you. At least he did things every now and again."

"What things?" asked Chuck.

"Well, he bought me bus tickets," said the Princess gloomily. "And if he was here, he'd carry me over to that island."

"River's pretty swift," said Chuck. "Probably kind of deep in the middle."

"Oh blow," said the Princess. "What a pioneer! I'll bet your people never got out to California until they'd invented the airplane. I'll go myself." She stood up and scooped up the ends of her skirt and stepped off into the river. The bottom was stony and she floundered around, staggering and exclaiming at the sharpness of the stones, but going forward nevertheless. She came to a deep hole and went up to her waist in it and then floundered out and Chuck sat on the bank grinning at her.

This annoyed the Princess who was now very wet indeed and she tossed her head and, still clinging to her dripping skirts, stumbled further out into the river. But Chuck was right and the channel between the bank and the island was very deep. The Princess went on for a few paces, stepped into the channel, and disappeared from sight.

Chuck dashed into the river after her, very angry, hopping on the stones. He ran down stream in the shallow part past the point where the Princess had disappeared and then floundered toward the center of the river and caught sight of her, struggling in the channel. He could swim pretty well but this wasn't the kind of water for swimming in. He grabbed at her as she went past and got her by the neck of the jumper she was wearing and hauled her into the shallows. Then he picked her up and carried her ashore.

He sat her down on the bank and shook her by the shoulders and said, "Are you all right?"

"Of course I'm all right," said the Princess, who indeed didn't seem to be much the worse for her accident. Then she shook the water out of her cropped hair, and smiled sweetly at him.

"That was rather nice of you," she said, wringing the water out of her skirt, quite prettily.

"You little minx," said Chuck. "I bet you did it on purpose."

"Of course I did it on purpose," said the Princess. "I was trying to help you. For a moment you were almost not stuffy. Almost knightly, in fact."

"Knightly?" said Chuck.

"Yes. Lancelot du Lac," said the Princess.

"Your head's full of that romantic nonsense," said Chuck. "Listen, there wasn't any Lancelot du Lac, no Arthur, nor Guinevere, nor Isolde the Fair. I've been studying it for two years and I know."

"There was too," said the Princess. "And there was a river like this with a little island in the middle."

"Oh that," said Chuck and quoted:

> "A river wondrous wide and set therein an island
> Which did the waters part like an otter's head
> Sleek with light and wetness.
> And all about the joyous ripples
> Like stars deposed, did to their Mother Heaven
> Cry of delight upon the pleasant Earth. . . ."

"Where did you get that from?" asked the Princess.

"Llydriff of Snowden," said Chuck. "It is a poem he wrote on the Arthurian legend telling how Lancelot brought the bride Guinevere to the King. The end is missing. I have never been able to find it."

"Say some more," said the Princess softly.

"Well, she fell in the river . . ."

"No. I mean poetry."

"Oh . . .

"Then put he the Lady Guinevere upon the bank
And seeing upon her face the trembling drops
As fresh as God's first morning on the earth
Kissed her. And forgot the King whose knight
    he was
Bound by vows before St. Edward's altar."

He bent over the Princess and she raised her face towards him and pulled him closer.

They did not hear the King approach. He stood and looked at them with infinite sadness, thinking of another love, long long ago, a love as lonely and forbidden as this one. The memory of it wrenched at him like the opening of an old wound and he bowed his head in anguish, so sharp was the pain, and went slowly away.

Chapter Sixteen

THE NATIONALIZED HORSE, BCH 224 FVO, on which the King, as noted, had ridden at a hand gallop to the convent, had been in the care of Farmer John Biggins, who, under the Land Use and Horse Control Act, had been given the horse to look after by the Ministry of Agriculture.

Under the terms of the appropriate section of the ordinance, Farmer Biggins was to have five pounds a week for keeping the horse on his land, and a remission of two hundred pounds in his income tax yearly. The horse was, therefore, more valuable to him useless than if he had been permitted to put it to work, which of course he was not.

But also under the same ordinance, Farmer Biggins was required to report to the police if the horse were removed from his property or if it strayed or if he observed anyone attempting to hitch it to a cart, plough, agricultural instrument of any kind, or lead it around the field by a halter (it had been ruled that the horse might be led by the mane without any violation of the ordinance), or attempt to mount it, straddle it, sit upon it, or ride it, with or without saddle and other harness.

When the King then went off with the horse, an open violation of the ordinance had obviously been perpetrated. But Farmer Biggins did not report this immediately.

One reason was that he was busy getting in the hay crop and, with rain threatening, he considered this his most important task. Again, he postponed making his report because of the number of forms which he knew he would be required to fill out. He didn't like filling out forms, and especially did not relish the task of filling out these particular reports because of the remarkable circumstances attaching to the person who had mounted the horse and ridden it off. The most remarkable of these circumstances being that the culprit had been clad head to foot in armor.

Finally, with the hay crop in and being in danger of fine for not making his report on the abuse and abduction of the horse in the time stipulated, he went down to the police station which was in a village two miles away and reported to the desk sergeant.

"Bloke took that 'orse that I'm looking after for the government," he reported to the sergeant.

The sergeant reached mechanically for a set of forms and pushed them to Farmer Biggins who took them with a sigh. He then got a pencil and wetted the point with his tongue and sweating somewhat from the effort, and with many glances out of the window for inspiration and at the sergeant for encouragement, filled the forms out.

The sergeant took the forms and read them through.

" 'Wearing a suit of armor,' " he read aloud when he got to this point of the form, "that makes it pretty serious."

"You mean they got something about that in the regulations?" asked the farmer.

The sergeant reached for a dog-eared book and after some rummaging through it started reading. " 'Section 127, subsection j,' " he read. " 'Anyone mounting a 'orse in a 'ostile manner shall be subject to a further fine of five pounds.' I'd say armor were 'ostile, I would."

He turned to the forms which the farmer had filled out and said, "I see the 'orse is over at the convent now. I'd better send a man along and make inquiries."

He sent a rural constable who returned in a couple of hours with the remarkable news that the horse was indeed at the convent, that it was claimed by a man who said he was King Arthur, that there was another man with him by the name of Cibber Brown from Glastonbury, who asserted that the man in the suit of armor was indeed King Arthur, and that furthermore there was a girl at the convent who said she was the Princess Pamela, and a young man at the convent who backed this assertation and had threatened to punch him (the constable) in the nose.

"They must all be barmy," said the sergeant on receiving this news. "Why didn't you bring back the 'orse?"

"I were going to do that," said the constable, "but this man in armor got on its back—jumped on he did, armor and all, like a acrobat—took 'is spear and run me out of the place."

"Barmy and dangerous," said the sergeant and considered what he should do. He did not consider long, but after a few moments called up the Home for Exceptional Adults and requested that a psychiatrist be sent to the convent in the company of the constable to certify two lunatics who had taken refuge there and have them admitted to the lunatic asylum.

"You mean the Home for Exceptional Adults," said the girl who took the message primly. "The name lunatic asylum is no longer authorized."

"Right," said the sergeant. "The nut house."

The psychiatrist then called at the convent in the evening of the same day, bringing with him four men since he had been warned that some resistance was to be expected especially from the man who called himself King Arthur. But the resistance he met with was not of the kind he had anticipated.

He found the King and interviewed him and the others in the parlor of the convent, in the presence of the aged Reverend Mother. The King insisted that he was King Arthur. The young girl insisted that she was the Princess Pamela and would not submit to being taken to the lunatic asylum or the Home of Exceptional Adults, as it was euphemistically called.

"I am afraid that I must take you to the Home," said the psychiatrist firmly. "It is my duty."

At this point Arthur intervened.

"You cannot take her away from here by force," he said slowly and gravely. "That is forbidden. The Princess is in a place dedicated to the service of God. She has claimed sanctuary here and the sanctuary afforded her is God's protection of His creatures. In this place, you harm her or force her to leave at the peril of your immortal soul."

There being nothing in the training of the psychiatrist to suggest that he had an immortal soul, or that anyone else had one for that matter, he gave a thin smile and was about to turn to the men with him to tell them to take the King away, but King Arthur stopped him with a gesture of his hand and continued what he was saying.

"It is an ancient law," he said, "not merely of this kingdom but of all Christendom that none of God's creatures who take refuge in such a place as this may be harmed in any way. This is true of the hare pursued by the hounds, or the hart by huntsmen, or unicorns whose mortal enemies are maidens and lions, and also griffins, which may be hunted with success only by two wizards, one of them being deaf so that his eyesight is of the finest, and the other dumb so that his hearing is acute."

"How could they communicate with each other with such handicaps?" asked the psychiatrist deciding to humor him.

"By the rearrangement of the stars in the sky," replied the King quietly. "The art has been lost. Merlin was the last one who could achieve it."

"Utter nonsense," said the psychiatrist, forgetting his training for the moment.

"You do not then believe that a star left its appointed place in the firmament to guide the Magi to the birthplace of Christ?" asked the King quietly and to this the psychiatrist could give no answer.

The King looked at the Princess. "If it is your wish, my lady," he said, "I will defend you, though I lack a sword."

He looked around, spied a large poker which stood by the fireplace and took this. " 'Tis a poor blade," he said, "but it will serve."

He now turned to the psychiatrist. "Of what station are you," he said, "that I may know whether it is mete that I should engage you in combat, or whether it would be more fitting to kick you out?"

"Civil Servant First Class Pensionable," said the psychiatrist who was rapidly losing his nerve.

"I doubt that is the equivalent of Knight," said the King

dubiously. "On the other hand," he added, eying the poker, "this is not the equivalent of a sword and so I will not dishonor myself by using it on you."

Here Chuck intervened and offered to serve the psychiatrist in the same manner he had offered to serve the policeman—namely by punching him in the nose, if he laid a hand on the Princess.

But the Princess said she didn't mind in the least going to the lunatic asylum, so long as Chuck was with her.

They were then taken away but not before the King had a private word with Cibber Brown.

"Go to my people in Glastonbury beyond the Forest Sauvage, churl," he said. "Tell them where their Princess is being taken."

"Yes, Your Highness," said Cibber, and it was the first time that he had used this term of deference to the King.

"If you should meet Merlin on the way, as I do not doubt that you will, he will explain to you some magic whereby this news can be made known to the people on the moment."

When the psychiatrist and the two policemen had departed to the lunatic asylum with King Arthur, Princess Pamela and Chuck, Reverend Mother went alone to her study to think over this development and to ponder her own position and that of the nuns under her care and guidance.

She had seen many strange developments in a life which, spanning eighty years, was not yet fully run. One of the strangest of them was that the only man who in the last two score years had offered to champion her and the nuns had been pronounced a lunatic.

When she had first come to the convent as a young woman, the convent had supported an orphanage.

This work could no longer be done.

It was not explicitly forbidden. The government had established certain regulations concerning the amount of living space which had to be given to each orphan, the amount of recreation area per child, the number of beds which might be put in a dormitory and the kind of clothing with which they should be provided, as well as the hours of their schooling, and the number of lay teachers who were to be employed per child and their payment, and so on. As the regulations mounted and multiplied, the expenses of running the orphanage multiplied and the sources of her revenue dwindled. People heavily taxed to support government plans had little left over to give to the convent.

And so the orphanage went.

In plain fact, she had lived to see the day when Christian charity had become a function of government, forbidden individuals, and religious organizations.

"It's almost as if no one can gain heaven unless they're in the British Civil Service," she said.

Her reveries were interrupted by the ringing of the bell at the front door, and after a short interval one of the nuns knocked at the door of her study.

"Come in," said Reverend Mother.

"It's the building inspector," said the nun.

The building inspector entered, wearing a raincoat and carrying a bowler hat—as much the uniform of his calling as the habit and wimple and coif was that of the nuns.

"I'm sorry to have to say this, ma'am," he said, "but the heating arrangements in this convent don't fulfill the code for the protection of health."

"But we're not here to protect our health so much as to serve God," said Reverend Mother.

"We've got nothing against that, ma'am," said the inspector, "provided you maintain a temperature of 68° Fahrenheit and no more than twenty pounds of pressure in the boilers. You will have to pull out that one old boiler and put in two new ones."

"We cannot install two new boilers," said Reverend Mother. "We have not the money."

"That's not my problem," said the building inspector. "I'll send you written notice of this, but I thought I'd come round and tell you myself first."

"That was kind of you," said Reverend Mother. "I have only one request to make."

"What is it?"

"Please send your notice to the lunatic asylum. I am taking the nuns there. I have no doubt the temperature is right and the boiler pressure correct in that place, and God, thank God, is everywhere."

Cibber, meanwhile, had climbed into the Rolls and driven off.

He had not gone very far when he met the RAC man who had helped to repair the car when it was broken down. The RAC man in his neat blue uniform was standing beside his motorcycle and side car and Cibber pulled over and stopped by him. The patrolman saluted and Cibber noted a look of secret amusement in his eyes.

"Not having any more trouble I hope, sir," said the patrolman.

Cibber had been uncertain from the time of their first acquaintance whether the patrolman was indeed Merlin. Some secret voice urged him not to ask the question directly but to ascertain the answer by some subtle means.

"Not car trouble," he said, "but I've got a problem."

"Perhaps I can help," said the patrolman in the friendliest way, the merriment now positively dancing in his eyes.

Now, said Cibber to himself, I can test him. If this is Merlin he will do some feat of magic whereby everybody in Britain will know on the moment that the Princess has been lodged in the Home for Exceptional Adults.

"My problem is to tell everybody that the Princess Pam has been put in the lunatic asylum," he said.

"I'd use the wireless and the newspapers if I were you, sir," said the patrolman to Cibber's disappointment. "And I'd telephone. There's a kiosk just up the crossroads." And then he got on his motorcycle, kicked the starter and drove off and Cibber was sure that he was laughing joyously.

Cibber went to the telephone and called the regional offices of the British Broadcasting Corporation in Glastonbury and reported the whereabouts of the Princess.

He had to call three times before he could convince whoever answered that he was not intoxicated. And then a dubious news editor said he would send a reporter to the home to check on the story. The reporter was sent, secured an interview with the Princess, was assured by the psychiatrist after the interview that such cases of self-delusion were not exceptional, and was further informed that the Princess had been in the company of a man who was clad in a suit of armor and insisted that he was King Arthur and was searching for his sword, Excalibur. The reporter returned thoughtfully to report to his chief in Glastonbury.

It had been a dull day for news. The principal item was an unconfirmed report that the tiny Duchy of Grand Fenwick had succeeded in landing a man on Mars and was laying claim to the planet. The news editor did not like stories concerning the inmates of lunatic asylums, but he thought he might put out a squib about the man in armor as being a somewhat unusual case.

The squib merely stated the facts—that an armored man who claimed to be King Arthur had been admitted to the local Home for Exceptional Adults in the company of a young girl who asserted that she was the Princess Pamela. It was broadcast on the ten o'clock news on the West of England broadcast, and rebroadcast on the Home Counties program from the BBC headquarters in London.

Both the High Commissioner of Scotland Yard and the Prime Minister caught the item. The PM went immediately to the Queen, in great distress, and the High Commissioner called

Broadcasting House and said that if the item were rebroadcast, he would see to it that the whole news staff was imprisoned for treason.

He then, also, went to the palace.

Chapter Seventeen

THE NEWSPAPERS pounced on the story like a hungry tiger on raw meat.

PRINCESS HELD INSANE, yelled the *Daily Mirror*.

ROYAL HEIR JUDGED LUNATIC trumpeted the *Daily Express*.

PRINCESS PAMELA COMMITTED TO ASYLUM thundered the *Daily Mail*.

Extras poured out as fast as the composing rooms could provide them, each with more and more details, so that the Prime Minister, consulting with the Queen and her consort, was driven to distraction by the continuous arrival of couriers carrying newspapers with bigger and bigger headlines and more and more appalling news.

Although it was close to midnight when the first extra came out in London, a mob had soon gathered around Buckingham

Palace, a tense multitude of people who stood there waiting for news from their queen about their princess. The mob was all the more menacing because there was no shouting or rioting or demonstrating. It was a huge, insistent presence, to which the Queen and her consort had to appear three times in half an hour. They were cheered and when the cheering died down came the shout, "Where is the Princess? Let us see the Princess."

The Prime Minister, using a hastily erected microphone and broadcast system, finally came to the balcony to assure the mob that the Princess was in no danger, that she had not been committed to a lunatic asylum, but was well and happy and of sound mind. Improvising as he went, for he was a man of some nerve in a crisis, he stated that the Princess had merely decided to visit the asylum as a work of personal charity and stay there for some days to study at first hand the operations of the institution. Her visit had been completely misinterpreted by the press. He had not the details of how this misinterpretation came about. He promised the people a full statement on the morrow and promised them that the Princess would be back in London on the morrow also. He advised the people in the crowd to go to their beds as there was no reason at all for their anxiety, and their presence, though understandable, was disturbing to the Queen.

This also was the attitude he took with his cabinet, summoned hastily to a meeting at the palace. The various members of the cabinet pressed him mercilessly for further information, and in the end he had to confess that he had received from the Princess a letter of resignation, stating that she did not like the restrictions upon her life entailed in the job of being princess, nor the prospects which lay before her as heir to the throne, and she hoped that someone more suitable might be found to fill the position.

"Do you suppose," asked the Minister of Health, "that the verdict of the psychiatrist in Somerset may be correct, and that the Princess may indeed be insane?"

"Nonsense," barked the Prime Minister.

"You mean that being of sane and sound mind she did not wish to be heir to the throne of England?" asked the Home Secretary. "It seems to me that the proper thing to do, to protect the prestige of the throne in the eyes of the people, would be to declare the Princess . . . er . . . not entirely sound in mind. Otherwise we go before the public and the world with an admission that nobody of sane mind would want to become Queen of England. That would be a disastrous blow."

"The Americans would never recover from it," said the Foreign Secretary. "They are devoted to royalty."

"I am not going to leave the Princess Pamela in a lunatic asylum as a concession to the feelings of the people in the United States of America," barked the Prime Minister. "We have made concessions enough in that quarter. She is to be brought back here to the palace and the whole thing explained as a piece of bungling on the part of *your* department" (glaring at the Minister of Health). "You'll have to resign, of course. I will express my regrets, pay tribute to your long public service, and I think I can promise you a peerage when the whole thing has simmered down."

"What troubles me," said the Archbishop of Canterbury,

who was present, though not himself a member of the cabinet, "is what happens if and when we do get the Princess back. If she has been dissatisfied in the past, she may quite reasonably be expected to be dissatisfied in the future. What we have to do is to find out what is the cause of her dissatisfaction, and do what we can to remove this cause."

"I understand from the Lady Beatrice," said the Chancellor of the Duchy of Lancaster, "that the Princess was constantly required to read Wordsworth. Perhaps that had something to do with it."

"Bah," snorted the Premier. "I survived Wordsworth. We all did. My proposal is that I and the Archbishop of Canterbury go to the Princess tonight and bring her back to the palace. The presence of the Archbishop will discount any suggestions by the leftist press of coercion."

"We may well have to make some concessions to the Princess to persuade her to return," said the Archbishop. "It might be advisable to consider what those concessions should be."

"How are we to consider them if we do not know what her grievances are?" asked the PM.

"In her letter," said His Grace, "she speaks of the restrictions of her life. I would take that to mean that there is far too much supervision and organization of her days so that she is incapable of viewing herself as an individual. There might be some lessening here."

The conference continued until dawn. It was finally agreed that the Prime Minister and the Archbishop would go to Somerset to interview the Princess and persuade her to return to the palace and her position. He would make what concessions he thought reasonable to bring this about. The Queen and the Prince Consort wished to accompany him, but the Prime Minister persuaded them that it would be better for them to remain in London. If they also went to Somerset it would only suggest to the nation that the crisis concerning the Princess was more real than they had been led to believe by the Prime Minister's explanation—an explanation which was now, of course, being published in the newspapers and broadcast on the wireless.

He then, with the Archbishop of Canterbury, went to see the Princess and, in the course of the drive to Somerset, he composed a document which he intended the Princess should sign so that he could immediately release it to the BBC and the press.

The document read:

Her Royal Highness Princess Pamela wishes it to be known that she had left the palace privately in order to visit the inmates of the Government Home for Exceptional Adults near Glastonbury. Her Highness has long felt a great interest in helping these people and in studying the techniques used in treating them and for this reason decided to spend some time at the home. She is much distressed that such an utterly false construction should be placed upon a personal act of charity which she believed quite in keeping with her position. She is grateful for the concern shown by the people of Britain over her welfare and deeply grieved that they should have been put through such an harassing experience as a result of an unfounded story.

Her Highness wishes to assure the people not only of the United Kingdom, but also of the sister nations of the

Dominions as well as the people of the British Empire, that she is in excellent health both physically and mentally and is returning to the palace to assume her normal life and duties.

When he had finished composing this message, the Prime Minister, somewhat uncharitably, woke up the Archbishop, who was snoozing in the back of the car beside him, and read it to His Grace. The Archbishop reacted with a sharp, ecclesiastical sniff.

"You're not very encouraging," grumbled the Premier.

"I don't think she'll sign it," said His Grace.

"Why not?" demanded the Premier.

"First because it is an utterly false statement," said the Archbishop, "and secondly because it treats her as if she was a minion of yours, as if she had no will of her own. From now on, I'm afraid you are going to have to get used to dealing with the Princess as an individual rather than as a piece of public property. By the way, do you think I look like a one-shilling bus ticket?"

"Yes," said the Prime Minister savagely. "Now that I come to think of it, you do. Why?"

"I learned from the young officer who used to wait on the Princess that she thought of me in this peculiar light," said the Archbishop. "She also thinks that you're a wowser."

"A wowser?" repeated the Premier. "What's a wowser?"

"Well, it's a cross between a sticky beak and a toe-ragger with some topoff thrown in," said the Archbishop. "In short, a spoilsport of the Mrs. Grundy type."

The Prime Minister reflected gloomily on this for the rest of the journey.

He had hoped to be able to interview the Princess by herself, but she refused to see him except in the company of several others. These several others included a ditch digger named Cibber Brown who seemed to be the personal servant of a lunatic who thought he was King Arthur, a somewhat pugnacious young American called Chuck Manners (the Prime Minister recalled him as the driver of the van in which he suspected the Princess had escaped from the palace) and a religious who had taken up her abode, with her nuns, at the lunatic asylum; her convent having been shut down because the temperature was not the correct one, according to the Ministry of Health, in which God might be served and worshiped.

Faced with the demand that all these be present the Prime Minister began to experience some misgivings about the state of the Princess' mind, and wondered whether the psychiatrist who had committed her to the lunatic asylum had not, after all, been right. He consulted with the psychiatrist who now completely reversed himself and said that the Princess was, without a doubt, in her right mind, but that he himself was experiencing some symptoms of derangement and was looking for someone to commit him to the very place of which he was the supervisor. The Prime Minister said he could arrange this as it would fall in nicely with government plans, providing an additional excuse, if needed, for the presence of the Princess in the home.

Defeated, however, by the insistence of the Princess that

these others be present at their interview, he finally had to give way. They were seated around a table in the large study of the director of the institution (who was busy drawing up his own papers of committal) and the Prime Minister got immediately to the point by producing the draft of the statement he had composed and asking the Princess to agree to it.

The Princess read the statement over carefully. Her face went pink with anger, and she threw the statement down on the table and said that it was a pack of lies and she would never agree to its being issued.

"But Your Highness," expostulated the Prime Minister, "I must have your agreement to this statement. Without it what explanation am I to offer the people for your presence here?"

"Tell them the truth," retorted the Princess, "that I resigned because I didn't like the job."

"That is unthinkable," said the Premier. "No word of such an explanation can ever be allowed to reach the public. You do not seem to appreciate what is at stake here—the succession to the throne—the whole future of the British monarchy—the prestige and dignity of the Crown. You must recall that from childhood you have been raised with every possible advantage to fulfill your rightful position as heir to the throne. You have had the advantage of the best education, of travel and the love and loyalty of your people. You owe it to the people to return to the duties which they look upon you to perform."

"Visiting goloshes factories and having lunch at canteens?" said the Princess. "Opening art shows and aviaries and dining with some of the most boring men in Europe? Being so much possessed that I don't own a piece of myself? No. Never!"

"I am sure," ventured the Archbishop, "that there can be a relaxation of this regimen. The matter has already been discussed in the cabinet and it is the consensus that too much of your life has, perhaps, been taken from you and you should be allowed more freedom as an individual."

Cibber Brown perked up at this and said in his West Country drawl, "Maybe 'twould be possible to borrow a public spade and go rabbiting and not get hauled into court."

"What the devil has that got to do with it?" demanded the Prime Minister.

"It's got a lot to do with it," said Cibber and related how he had been arrested for taking the spade.

"I don't follow you at all," snapped the Prime Minister.

"I do," said Reverend Mother Gabriel. "It is like having to worship God at a temperature of 68 degrees Fahrenheit. I don't know the Centigrade equivalent."

"Or riding a horse without a government license," put in the King.

"This is all roaring nonsense," said the Prime Minister.

"No," said the Archbishop, "it is not. These are somewhat bizarre examples, but none the less fitting, of the extent to which people's individual lives have become controlled by government restrictions, from the highest to the lowest in the land. Something must be done about removing these restrictions. The Princess has dramatized them by her flight and resignation. The result has been that she was committed to this asylum."

"That is not fair," said the Prime Minister. "She was put here in error, as you well know, Your Grace."

"An error on the part of the government," said the Archbishop. "Let us not forget that. I think we should acknowledge that the Princess has some good cards in her hands if she wishes to play them. Let us acknowledge that we are prepared to have her return to the palace on her own terms, within reason. And those terms will include an easement, not only on the restrictions upon herself, but upon all in the kingdom, since I assume that those here are her friends and that would be her desire."

All now looked hopefully at the Princess, but the Princess shook her head.

"No," she said. "I will not go back."

"But you cannot throw aside the loyalty and love of your people in this manner," cried the Prime Minister.

"I seek only the love and loyalty of one person," said the Princess, looking at Chuck. The Prime Minister looked at him too, a hard and angry look. The Archbishop groaned openly. The King looked at Chuck also, with great sadness, as if gazing on an old sorrow which had never given him rest.

"Young man," said the Prime Minister, "I would like a word with you in private." Chuck nodded and they went together into the adjoining room.

"Now," said the Prime Minister when they were alone, "I am not going to inquire closely into what relationship or understanding you may think you have established with Her Royal Highness. But you must realize that this is merely a transitory matter, and in any case, an impossible matter. When the time comes, Her Royal Highness must make a suitable match for the good of the people. You will play no part in that. I expect you to leave this place and not return. I will explain to the Princess that you have gone and no longer entertain any personal feeling for her."

"I won't," said Chuck.

"I want to point out to you," said the Prime Minister, "that your position is not an enviable one. There are certain charges which might be brought against you in regard, shall I say, to the abduction of the Princess—charges which I do not think Her Majesty's Government would have much difficulty in substantiating—and which would carry the direst penalties for yourself. I would advise you to think your situation over and at the same time reflect on the service you can perform by leaving now so that this monstrous error on the part of the Princess may be corrected. If you do as I say and leave, there will of course be no question of any charges being brought against you."

"No," said Chuck. "I'm staying."

"If you had any real love for the Princess, you would leave," said the Prime Minister.

"If you knew what love was," replied Chuck, "you wouldn't ask."

"Very good," said the Prime Minister and they returned to the conference room. Here the Prime Minister excused himself while he whispered to the Archbishop and the two of them then withdrew.

"What did he want?" asked the Princess.

"He wanted me to walk out on you—cold," said Chuck.

"Maybe that would have been best," said Cibber slowly, studying his hands.

"Chuck and I are meant for each other," said the Princess quickly.

"If you are," said Reverend Mother, "then you have nothing to fear."

The Prime Minister and the Archbishop now returned. The Archbishop now tackled the Princess, urging her to return to her duties and pointing out that she was consecrated to the service of the people and could not turn her back upon her duties, and leave England, on the death of her sister the Queen, without a direct heir to the throne. He pointed out how ancient was the institution of monarchy in England, that it had survived for over a thousand years, that it had in all that time united the people in a living symbol of their country which could, at one and the same time, be loved and reverenced.

But the Princess was as adamant at the end of his plea as she had been at the beginning. She did not want to be a princess any more. She had resigned that position and wished now only to be allowed to live the life of a private individual.

There was silence then. Nobody knew what to say further. Argument had proved of no avail. What was needed, the Prime Minister and the Archbishop sensed, was not argument but some dramatic development which, by its very impact, would shake the Princess' determination.

Cibber Brown looked miserably at his hands. The Prime Minister examined the surface of the table. The Archbishop, head bent, plucked at one eyebrow in deep thought. In the silence, the King rose and said, "I beg you let me speak to these two alone. Let only the Lady Abbess remain besides."

Chuck did not know what to make of this man who called himself King Arthur. He had never known what to make of him since they first met. He had thought of him originally as an English eccentric, but there was too much to his presence; too much dignity and indeed greatness, for such a glib explanation. Sometimes he thought of him not so much as a man in the physical sense, but as a presence, a continuing embodiment of some ancient English heritage. He thought of him in this way now that they were alone with him. Seeking to get on firmer ground with him he asked:

"Who *are* you, anyway?"

"If you think deeply you will remember all," was the reply. Who had said that or something similar before? Chuck wondered. The RAC patrolman. He had said that Chuck would have no difficulty with his dissertation about the Arthurian legend because if he thought, he would remember a great deal he had forgotten. And there was some other connection here. The Princess had said at their first meeting that she had known him before. It seemed to Chuck now that this was true; that he had somewhere at some other time met both this man and the Princess. But he could not recall the meeting. He had a feeling that it had taken place but no picture of it.

"I cannot remember what you are asking me to remember," he said.

"A river with an island like an otter's head," said the King.

"Go on," said Chuck. He was tense and nervous, as a man is who walks into a long-forgotten dwelling.

> "Then put he the Lady Guinevere upon the bank
> And seeing upon her face the trembling drops
> As fresh as God's first morning on the earth
> Kissed her. And forgot the King whose knight
>   he was
> Bound by vows before St. Edward's altar . . ."

"And the rest?" Chuck asked, his breath coming so hard he could scarcely get the words out.

"A prophecy," said the King.

"What is it?"

> "These twain shall meet again at Camelot
> And then they shall renew their love of old
> Or faithful to their vows sworn long before
> Part . . ."

The King stopped and the three stood in silence for a while.

"There is more," said the King at length. "Do you not recall it now?"

"No," said Chuck, but he was not speaking the truth, for he now remembered the last lines but was afraid to say them because of his love for the Princess.

"I will tell them to you," said the King gently.

> "Which if they do not part
> No more king shall be in Inglelonde
> And all her glories turned to commonness
> As happened when these two first did meet
> And love in Arthur's time."

Chuck heard the Princess catch her breath. She rose and walked to the window and stood looking out of it, and remained there for a long time. She had her back to him, and without looking around she said finally in so small a voice that he could scarcely catch the words:

"Goodbye, Sir Knight. And God be with you."

When she turned he had gone and his absence made the room so empty that her eyes filled with tears.

Reverend Mother now rose, and as she did so the crucifix which she wore in the bodice of her habit caught the beam of sunlight coming through the window and glowed so brightly that its light seemed to fill the whole room, as if some golden sword of huge size, and emitting a radiance of its own, stood for a moment before them.

"What is it?" asked the Princess, trembling.

"Excalibur," said the King. "The end of my quest and the beginning of yours."

Chapter Eighteen

SIR TIMOTHY had been having the dullest time of it in his dungeon at Camelot. He kept pleading to be allowed to see King Arthur and being assured that King Arthur had been lured into the Forest Sauvage by necromancy, and that he was to be kept a hostage for the King's safe return.

He was beginning to lose all memory of mortal time, though occasionally in his dreams he had nightmares in which he was filling out a ten-page income tax return or arguing with a government clerk at the Personnel Bureau whether his occupation should be listed as "nobleman" or "unemployed."

What was worse was that two wyverns had been put in the dungeon with him. They were peaceable enough reptiles but they suffered heavily from halitosis, and they liked to carry on long conversations with each other debating the conditions of wyvern neo-existence.

At first this discussion of neo-existence bothered Sir Timothy because he could make no sense of it. But gradually he discovered that wyverns belonged to a neo-existing order of reptiles of which the chief were dragons and the lowest jeweled salamanders, who live in the heart of fires and have a precious stone set in the center of their heads. Anyone who can snatch a jeweled salamander out of the heart of the fire may have the precious stone.

"I can't say that I understand all this very much," said Sir Timothy to one of the wyverns. "It seems to me that either you exist or you don't exist, but to pretend there is a third state called neo-existence seems complete balderdash to me."

"That's because you're still troubled by remnants of mortality," said one of the wyverns, a female running to fat in her tail and rather disturbed about it.

"If you'll just explain to me I'll listen very carefully," said Sir Timothy. "Only don't come any nearer, please."

"Well," said the wyvern, "you have to consider existence. Think about it for a few years and then we will start our discussion."

"But I'm incapable of thinking of anything for more than a minute or so at a time," pleaded Sir Timothy.

"You poor thing," said the wyvern. "You must be not quite dead."

"Oh yes, I'm dead all right," Sir Timothy said cheerfully. "But the habit of a lifetime of letting my thoughts jump from subject to subject still persists. I'll start off thinking about existence and that will remind me that much of my hair has ceased existing because I am getting bald, and then I will wonder whether there isn't something that can be done to prevent baldness, and then I'll wonder why few women go bald, and then I'll think of a woman with a lot of hair and that leads me straight to Hottentots, and that's a long way from existence where I started."

The wyvern sighed.

"Then I can do very little for you," she said and started to hum a little tune, making a noise like a bass viol being bowed on its lowest string with rather too much rosin on the bow.

"I think your tail is quite elegant," said Sir Timothy, inspired.

"Flattery will get you nowhere," said the wyvern though she gave a little hiss of pleasure. "I am altogether overweight."

"I like a tail that is substantial," said Sir Timothy hopefully, "it gives a wyvern presence."

"Thank you," said the wyvern, and her scales which were normally a silver-blue, turned saffron with pleasure.

"About neo-existence," the wyvern continued, "there are creatures which exist, which is to say that they go through a state of mortal life, and then there are creatures who never have mortal life though their presence is known by mortals and these are said to neo-exist. You don't really think that my tail is overplump, do you?"

"I would say without hesitation that you are a handsome figure of a wyvern," said Sir Timothy.

"I am inclined to agree with you, though I abominate flattery," said the wyvern and her scales now changed from saffron to an elegant shade of rose madder.

"Such neo-existing creatures are best known to the Celtic peoples among the inhabitants of Europe and include unicorns, winged horses (also giant white horses without wings), wyverns, dragons, griffins, and among humankind, authropophagi and cyclops (I am uncertain of the plural).

"Then there are Seraphim and Cherubim and Angels of varying degrees, also Dominations and Powers. And for the children there are leprechauns and pookas and sprites and djinns, and so on. I am sure that during your childhood as a mortal you must have seen pictures of these."

"Yes," said Sir Timothy. "Of course I was brought up at a time when all children's reading was not tediously directed toward their education and they were allowed and encouraged to read for sheer amusement."

"No one in whose mind there is not room for a wyvern or a griffin or a jeweled salamander is fitted for living," said the wyvern. "They lack an essential elasticity."

"Quite so," said Sir Timothy. "But now that you have explained to me about neo-existence could you kindly tell me what you are doing in the dungeon?"

"We are taking a holiday," said the wyvern.

"A holiday?" exclaimed Sir Timothy in surprise.

"Oh yes. When the King is at Camelot we are the supporters of his crest. But now that he is away we are permitted to luxuriate in this dismal, damp, dark dungeon, instead of being almost dehydrated in the blinding, horrible, healthful sunlight. I love the smell of mold, don't you? It reminds me of autumn decay and fills me full of the most glorious gloomy thoughts."

"I prefer spring flowers myself," said Sir Timothy.

"*De gustibus non est disputandum*," said the wyvern with a certain superiority.

"Do you know when the King will return?" asked Sir Timothy. The two wyverns looked at each other dismally.

"Almost any eon now," said the first of them.

"Perhaps not for ages," said the other.

"Only Merlin knows," said the first wyvern.

"And where is Merlin now?" asked Sir Timothy.

"In some far corner of a state called Time," the wyvern replied, weeping bitterly for happiness, for it must be clear by now that wyverns work in exactly the opposite manner to human beings, sobbing when they are happy and grinning when they are mournful.

"It is probable that he is lost there," one of them said and at this delightful prospect, promising an eternity of vacation for them in the dungeon, the two broke into floods of tears out of sheer joy.

Sir Timothy wept a little too, though of course for contrary reasons, and the wyverns were pleased to see him so sad.

"When will you know that Merlin has returned?" asked Sir Timothy.

"There will probably be a great flash of light and the whole of Camelot will be lifted thousands of miles up into the air and then put down again," said the first wyvern.

"Or there will be a terrible noise and the walls will shake so much that they will seem to be about to crumble to the ground," said the other. "But cheer up and have a piece of that delightfully moldy bread because it may not be for ages and ages."

The wyverns were wrong, however.

Suddenly there was a terrible sharp roaring noise and the door of the dungeon was flung open as if by magic (in fact it was magic) and Sir Timothy, rushing up the stairs and followed by the wyverns who were grinning with sorrow, saw a RAC patrolman wheel briskly into the courtyard on his motorcycle and side car.

"Merlin! Merlin!" cried Sir Timothy and ran to embrace him. "I'm awfully glad to see you."

"Always glad to be of service to members," said the RAC man saluting politely.

Behind the motorcycle was Sir Timothy's Rolls Royce with King Arthur at the wheel and all the knights and ladies of Camelot gathered around to inspect this new marvel of Merlin's and to greet their sovereign.

"What kind of an enchantment is this?" they asked, staring at the Rolls.

"It's a Rolls Royce," said Sir Timothy with pride and he added, for he was still a mite earthbound, "I don't think we can use it much because there isn't any petrol."

"I shouldn't worry about that if I were you, sir," said the RAC man. "It has a Merlin engine."

There is hardly much more to tell. Cibber Brown went back to Glastonbury and resumed his job as ditch digger, and a somewhat mysterious order emanating from the Ministry of Agriculture in London and directed through channels to his brother-in-law, Mr. Melton, made it clear that he was to be allowed to borrow a spade from the Rural District Council's toolshed any time he wanted to go rabbiting. Cibber was indeed offered a far better position, as supervisor of ditches, but he said he had no desire to be a supervisor and so took his old job. However, Bors House having come under government control as a national trust on the death of Sir Timothy, Cibber was appointed caretaker of the place and allowed to take up his residence in it.

People passing the place at night said that Cibber was heard to be carrying on conversations with Sir Timothy and so the story grew that the place was haunted and it is alleged to be haunted to this day.

Chuck completed his dissertation on the Arthurian legend, producing more authorities and more details than had ever been previously brought forward. He returned to Santa Barbara as a member of the faculty and was known among other things as one of the few men in the United States who maintained a personal correspondence with Princess Pamela, heir to the throne of England. He many times returned to England, visiting the convent and meeting the Princess there.

They would sit by the stream together, sometimes alone and sometimes with some of the nuns. Once, when her sister had died and the Princess became Queen Pamela the First and took a consort, the propriety of these visits with Chuck was questioned in the Privy Council. Queen Pamela replied by quoting the motto of one of the most ancient orders of Britain's knighthood, instituted by the King Edward III in imitation of the brotherhood of the Round Table.

"Honi soit qui mal y pense," she said, and the matter was never raised again.

The nuns, of course, returned to the convent, and as a result of the relaxation of the laws which had made charity an exclusive and jealously guarded function of government, were once again able to care for orphans and others in need as much of love and solicitude, as of clean clothes and regular meals. Reverend Mother was delighted that Christianity had been restored to the people instead of being a function of the government.

As for King Arthur, Merlin and Sir Timothy, they, as indicated, just disappeared and were never seen again.

That is, of course, unless one is prepared to give credence to the West Country stories that Cibber Brown and Sir Timothy were accustomed to holding midnight sessions in the older part of Bors House just outside Glastonbury—stories elaborated to the extent that some people passing reported that they could not only hear voices but smell rabbit pie cooking.